S0-BRE-539

MIS CEL LA·NE OUS

By:

Tristian

Ugalde

This is a work of fiction. Any references to people, places, or things currently living/dead/or in a state of dying, is entirely coincidental.

1

Guardados,
Thank you for
y our support and
I hope you enjoy this!
Sincerley,
J. W.
(your favorite
neighbor)

*For the rather wonderful group of people I
am proud to call friends.*

2

Acknowledgments

For any writer to ever claim that he completed a work without the support and encouragement of others, is a complete lie. Therefore I must thank all the following individuals:

(For those of you more interested see: *1 Peter 4:10-11*)

Alysa Evenson, with whom I had engaged in a conversation one night that would breed an idea and the idea itself, became this book which you now see before you. Without her, this might never have come into existence.

Rachel Seemann, my dear friend whose contributions to the original draft remain in the skeleton of this work. But also her encouragement from the very beginning only fueled my ambitions.

To Leila Bouanani, Dani Durr, Ryan Dycus, Kendra Gibble, Alex Kaprosy, Cristina Moraga, Ashley O'Dore, Phoebe Schultz-Smith, and Mrs. Liza Taylor all of whom read throughout the various drafts of the novel and offered their numerous corrections, praises, recommendations, and assistance throughout the book at its various stages. I find it hard to put into words exactly how truly thankful I am. Their help saw to this book's creation.

To Chandler Barteau for his own input in regards to the story and his wonderful book design! The visual appeal of this book would have suffered greatly had it not been for his talent.

There is also a numerous list of people that showed interest and offered encouragement all along the way: Calli Bagshaw, Kim Blystra, CJ Caron, Dr. Theresa Chavez, Kearsen Cochran, Ragan Cole, Keely Cutler, Tyler Daugherty, Thor Evans, Jelonni Goodson, Josh Harris, Brianna Hearn, Max Honebrink, Kyle Hunter, Karlyn Lantz, Ms. Judith McElhinney, Tristan Odenkirk, Kiersten Patterson, Tiffany Pham, Arron Pontbriand, Dominique Pulver, Bianca Reilly, James Rivera-Torres, Kayla Robbins, Anissa Sandoval, Ian Schneider, Emma Stambaugh, Cynthia Tjalas, Randi Tuffly, Brendon and Carly Vanderkolk, Tommy Wahl, Tee Ward, Sarah Washburn, Tessa White, Shane Wiegand, and Cole Wilson.

Most importantly my family, for their love and support, all the same. It would not have been possible to write this story if it was not for them.

Lastly, but certainly not least, I must thank both Louise Boost and Alexis Powers, the two ladies who run a local writers' motivational workshop. They-as well as the other lovely authors I have had the privilege of meeting-have been nothing but supportive ever since I presented this work. They are truly, a very miscellaneous group of people.

Author's note

Dear reader,

The content of this book is both highly critical and satirical. The purpose of satire through any sort of art is to bring about criticism of something (be it ideas, people, politics, religion, fields of study etc.) while simultaneously entertaining the audience. I will be the first to say that this novel does not seek to criticize people, but rather the flawed thinking that exists in the minds of many, however we all suffer from it. In order to accomplish this, I have drawn from situations and experiences that I have encountered in my own life. I have no intention of putting the blame on individuals, but rather on those seemingly stubborn ideals that lodge themselves in our heads throughout the course of history. Furthermore, I hope you enjoy all of it, just as much as I do.

Yours truly,

The author

She awoke; her head emitted a heavy throbbing, her vision was reduced to a blur. She was lying across a couch, still wearing her day clothes and a scant, white sheet had been draped over her body. The surrounding room appeared to be a modest apartment. The whole place was a wreck. Empty bottles and random strangers were strewn across the floor, asleep in fetal positions and curled into the various nooks and crannies. There was the strong stench of alcohol and the air was exceedingly cold.

Where the hell am I? Raquel Polanski could not remember anything of the previous night's activities. She shuffled off the small white sheet and relieved a small knot that had formed in the lower part of her back. The only thing Raquel noticed was a small window, revealing the better part of the New York skyline, amidst the first snowfall of the year. The sudden sound of footsteps caused her to whirl around only to come face-to-face with a young man, clad in soft, silk pajamas and carrying a steaming cup of coffee.

"Ah, I never thought you would awaken," the young man croaked out groggily, "All the others are still enjoying their New Year's Day slumber."

Raquel didn't even recognize him. "What happened?"

"Those hangovers are dreadful. I daresay you were probably the most taciturn person in New York City last night."

"New York City?"

"Oh dear. You don't remember anything, do you?"

Raquel solemnly shook her head.

"Must I explain the situation? I never did believe amnesia accompanied hangovers."

"Will you please just help me?"

"Why, most certainly." The young man finished his cup of coffee and flung the empty cup at a wall with a loud *SMASH!* The people on the ground didn't even flinch. "See, they are asleep in the soothing arms of liquor!" he smiled shyly.

"You were going to tell me what happened…"

"Ah, yes. Well, I decided that I might host a New Year's Party this year in my rather modest apartment, as you can see. I decided that everybody at the offices would appreciate such a party for I could not dare to think about inviting

11

my fellow tenants. They are people of the most dreadful breed: a trumpet player who practices at the most ungodly hours of night, some man, whom must be deaf, that watches his television at a ludicrous volume, and a couple whose clearly, audible trysts have devastated the quality of my sleep."

Raquel interrupted, "I think I get the picture."

"Well, lo and behold New Year's Eve was upon me and every invited person had arrived. You were the very last one to arrive and by that time, the entire apartment was so festive. You were rather reserved at first so I decided to introduce you to everyone I personally knew. There are many wonderful people at Ironwood Press I daresay…"

"Did I know anyone at the party?"

"A few of them said they had seen you around the offices when you arrived but you were peculiarly interested into that one fellow…I believe Christian is *his* name; a very courteous custodian fellow whom works at the offices. I am afraid that I cannot recall his last name."

In that moment, Raquel remembered everything: meeting the famous author, the whole party, crying "Happy New Year's!" at

Midnight, the vague familiarity of the janitor she had talked to…

The young man's voice dragged on in the background, "…of course by that time I had decided to retire from the festivities, but upon arriving in my bedroom, there was a young couple in my bed, intent on displaying their physical affection for one another." He gave a slight shudder. "So I took to the bathroom and proceeded to play Solitaire atop the commode until…"

"OH MY GOD! You're Christian Martinez!" The moment of revelation had begun.

Christian only shook his head solemnly. "Tsk, tsk. It seems as if the effects of the liquor are starting to recede."

"Oh my gosh, I remember meeting you, when you gave me that invitation at the farewell address…"

"Yes, yes. I can see that things are becoming quite clear for you now."

"And Christian! Oh my gosh I have to find him. Not you…I mean…the *other* Christian"

Christian only looked at her, puzzled. "Do you know our Mr. Custodian from somewhere Miss Polanski?"

"I can't explain right now Christian, it's a long story." Raquel was up and about in a flash. Within seconds she had located both of her shoes that had been hidden among the post-party floor.

Christian looked thoroughly confused. "Well if you are going to leave in such haste, remember to take your jacket. The weather outside is dreadful and..." But Raquel couldn't hear him; she had already disappeared out the door.

*   *   *

Humble Beginnings

Ironwood Press had started out as a modest publishing house, established in New York City right on the outskirts of the Financial District, in the *Tyler Hawke* building. The *Hawke* building was a drab piece of cubic concrete resembling a prison, measuring only ten stories-high the building was an ugly stigma among the glistening skyscrapers of Manhattan. For whatever reason, company founder Antonio Benjamin had decided to use the *Hawke* building as the headquarters for the newly established publishing house. It wasn't until he noticed the high rate of depression among the newly hired staff that a decision was made to paint the interior of the *Hawke* building. However, the colors were more horrendous than the original gray; they had become an interior decorator's worst nightmare.

The walls had been streaked with an arrangement of purple, turquoise, and light red stripes that covered the majority of the walls. "According to workplace psychologists you need brighter colors. They're supposed to enhance optimism and coworker cooperation." Mr. Benjamin had told his vice-CEO Mitchell Schuler when discussing changes that needed to be brought to the company.

Ironwood Press had vastly expanded within a period of only a few years. The company had become a powerhouse, generating sensational bestsellers and raking in income with figures that most fast-food chains found astounding. Upcoming and renowned authors alike began to amass into the company itself and soon, Ironwood Press could brag the works of authors such as the illustrious Margaret O'Neil, renowned children's illustrator Thomas Wallace, the insightful Cristina Muñez, and the vastly eccentric Christian Martinez.

"We need to start categorizing the authors." It was Schuler addressing Mr. Benjamin privately aboard the company yacht during a ten year anniversary celebration. Both of them were wearing finely tailored suits and drinking alcoholic beverages that had come from some God-only-knows-where corner of France and whose name most people had a hard time pronouncing, but the stuff was expensive and looked great in a glass. "It would certainly help with organization around the offices. Just think about it Tony; we'd have little departments, each one specializing in something. One for reporting sports, one for drama related materials, one for romance, one for self-help manuals...I mean...hell, we could have one for the writers who just don't belong anywhere. Imagine, we'd call it: The Miscellaneous Department." Schuler let out a little chuckle.

Mr. Benjamin simply stared out across the water and sighed. "You're a great friend Mitch, honest to God, you are. But I feel like that would only hurt the company. Just look at what we're producing right now. Our writers have no restrictions on the diffusion of ideas and just look at them go. I think we're heading in the right direction right now and I kinda want to keep it that way. I don't mean any disrespect Mitch. I really appreciate what you want for the company but I just don't feel that's the way things need to be just now."

Schuler only shrugged however he harbored a despicable amount of wrath on the inside. *Who the hell is this idiot to tell me what to do/* "It's just a suggestion."/*I do so much for this company and the bastard can't even appreciate my ideas/*"But yeah, no hard feelings."/*If **I** was in charge of this company maybe we'd be making a little more cash. We'd be making bank/* "Now how about me and you head inside and get more of that champagne?"

Interestingly enough, that was the same night Mr. Benjamin disappeared mysteriously from the company yacht and was tragically never seen again. No body was ever recovered. The story made headlines all across the North American Continent:

BELOVED PUBLISHING HOUSE CEO DISAPPEARS OFF YACHT DURING COMPANY PARTY. FRIENDS AND FAMILY CLAIM IT MAY HAVE BEEN SUICIDE.

"We're all really going to miss Tony; he was just such a great guy." Mitchell Schuler stated in one of his many interviews following the disappearance. "He was having a really hard time; being under a lot of stress and trying to see to the future of the company and it just got to the poor guy." Several days later a public statement from Schuler was released stating, "Out of respect for the late Tony Benjamin, Ironwood Press will be closed for the next week as a sign of mourning for the one man who made this company possible."

So time went on and Mitchell Schuler had become the new CEO of Ironwood Press and under his rule, things began to change. Schuler organized all the writers into various departments in order to "maintain relevant ideas in their relevant environments" (whatever that meant) and to "establish some organization around the offices". Sure enough, the authors organized themselves into little departments and no one thought anything of it, but as time progressed, they grew into factions. Each department was so set on its own ideals that they feared anything from the outside. Strange cases of departmental xenophobia begun to appear and no one knew what to do. Authors, who were once great friends, now abhorred each other. Years' worth of human relationships had been severed, all in the course of a few weeks. And then there were the few writers that raised hell.

A few of the writers had rebelled against the idea of the departments. Schuler simply responded with, "Well if you don't like it, leave." And some did. Others simply couldn't leave the company they had once been a part of for so long, so Schuler offered a compromise, "Since you can't simply assimilate yourselves into an existing department, I'll make you all your own department, and you can gripe and bitch there all you want." And they all took him up on the offer. Thus, the Miscellaneous Department of Ironwood Press was born. But of course the other departments thought of themselves as being superior to this new and obviously inferior department. And every poor human being at Ironwood Press thought of himself being greater than his neighbor, who in turn, thought the same thing about the original thinker.

Ironwood Press never did see the same fame and fortune that were an accented characteristic of those "Benjamin Years" as most authors liked to refer to it. "The Golden Age of the Press" some liked to call it jokingly. But Schuler would have none of it. He was the *best* CEO that Ironwood Press ever *had* and *was going to have*. However, company sales were plummeting and soon Schuler found himself desperately trying to quench the company's debt. He decided to open the doors to Ironwood Press for young, energized and enthusiastic writers who were still in the making. Newspaper ads and internet pop-ups lent themselves out to messages like:

Are You Interested in writing for a living? Ironwood Press can help you. To get in touch with one of our agents just click the link below...

Sure enough, the advertisements warranted plenty of reaction and young and aspiring authors, yearning to make a living, flocked to New York City; Ironwood Press being one of the few, if not the only publishing house that accepted stories to be published only *if* the person had an actual hardcopy manuscript that could be presented to the CEO himself. Many of the authors were awful and Schuler felt a tinge of pain as he rejected each one. Things seemed to be falling apart.

In the city of Tucson, Arizona, one young girl had stumbled upon the advertisements. Her name was Raquel Polanski and she had a manuscript, plenty of ambition and a head full of dreams and wishes to pursue after Ironwood Press' offer. All she lacked was money…

*   *   *

Ch. 2

As soon as Raquel felt the bite of frosty air, she regretted not heeding Christian's advice and grabbing the jacket. On the streets there was confetti and trash everywhere. The city was still ravished by the last night's festivities. People walked about drunkenly, still trying to successfully place on foot in front of another. A million faces walked with bloodshot and dark eyes. Raquel empathized deeply with everyone she passed. Personally, she had a ridiculous headache from probably being hung-over, but Raquel wasn't about to let that deter her from finding Christian the Janitor.

Waves of onrushing pedestrians forced Raquel to step off the curb and face the building she had just left. It was a large twenty story apartment complex and the thought of returning to the warm apartment was tempting. The cold was getting to her and she decided to find the nearest coffee shop and grab a quick pick-me-up while getting out of the cold.

Raquel entered a nearby coffee shop, which was virtually empty, and started to order. "One mocha latte with extra whipped cream and a turbo, please."

"Would you like a turbo shot or a double?" The minimum-waged barista with a name tag that read: **Kendall Prize** asked, not seeming like she really cared; no doubt thinking about all the other places she could be than in the Big Apple on New Year's Day making cheap pre-made lattes for hung over, depressed, and generally grouchy city dwellers who ordered drinks that were more cream and sugar than coffee.

Although it was a seemingly simple question, Raquel had to think hard. Kendall repeated the question twice before Raquel could answer.

"Better make it a double, I just need to wake up."

"That will be $3.14."

Raquel quickly dug into her pockets, rummaging for the last bit of her emergency change. She quickly took some out and handed it to Kendall. "Here you go."

"Thank you and have a Happy New Year."

Raquel made her way to an empty table in the corner and took a seat. She then proceeded to take a long gulp of her coffee which she instantly regretted; it burned and she knew things probably wouldn't taste correctly for the next week.

Where to start looking for that janitor Christian and why does he seem so familiar? Where do I even begin to look for clues? A sudden buzz from her phone reminded Raquel to check missed calls, emails, and new texts. There were no missed calls, no voicemails and only one new message from a friend, Sarah Burns, a friend who had moved out to New York and become a successful restaurant owner. The message simply read: Heard you were in the Big Apple. Want to get together some time soon? It wasn't exactly Raquel's top priority so she pushed the message aside and decided to look at emails. At first glance, there was nothing unusual: just the pointless newsletters she had signed up for on a spur-of-the-moment decision. There was also one from Mr. Schuler with the "policies of Ironwood Press and its employees." And then something caught her eye: a new message from christianarizonah@gmail.com. *What a strange address. Probably spam.* Right before she clicked on the message out of curiosity, the bell over the café entrance door rung, averting her attention from the email. Christian Martinez had just meandered in.

As he started to approach her, Raquel shrieked out, "What are you doing here? How did you find me? You're not one of those creeps are you?"

"Happy New Year to you as well, Miss Polanski." he mumbled.

Raquel couldn't decide if he was offended or just teasing her. "Sorry Christian, you had just surprised me, that's all." There was an awkward moment of silence before Raquel spoke again, "I was wondering why you came to find me."

Christian chuckled and began, "Because you asked, I felt it was only proper to return your jacket. I simply asked the building door man, Maximilian if he had seen a girl…and then I proceeded to describe you. Fortunately, Maximilian has a superior photographic memory and he directed me in this general direction. I saw the coffee shop and deduced, 'where would a cold, hung-over, young writer go for ideas and inspiration?'"

She had never thought of herself as being so predictable. "So where is the jacket?" Christian slowly unraveled the mass of leather that he had wound about his arm and handed over the coat. Raquel quickly slipped it on and welcomed the extra warmth.

"Why don't you grab a cup of coffee and join me awhile?" Raquel offered.

"Oh, I would be much obliged Miss Polanski." He left for the front counter while Raquel continued to stare down the strange message.

Christian returned to the table bearing a small saucer of coffee with cream and sugar. "So, have you discovered anything about our Mr. Janitor?" Christian asked while stirring sugar into his coffee.

"Well I found this really strange email that I was about to open right before you came in."

"Well proceed to read it; after all, the email may hold all the answers we need."

Raquel looked blankly at the email. It all felt so strange, especially when it came to thinking about *him*...

"Miss Polanski please open the email, the suspense is killing me." Christian had begun to vigorously stir his coffee, turning his spoon into a human-powered eggbeater.

Raquel snapped back to reality and clicked on the email. Her eyes scanned the email. She could hardly believe it; all the feelings from the past had rushed up again like an emotional tide that had receded after the end of a long, tumultuous love affair.

*   *   *

The Wait

After lots of begging, emotional manipulation, and flat out asking people for money, Raquel had finally earned herself a one-way ticket to New York City. Then Raquel spent an additional four hours (not including getting to and waiting at Tucson International) in a third class seat crammed along with screaming children and irritated parents. Then, she had arrived (thankfully) at JFK International with only her dreams, a suitcase that contained several articles of clothing and a manuscript, and enough money for cab-fare and a few nights at a really cheap hotel, if anything *cheap* were still in existence.

It took Raquel an additional thirty minutes trying to hail a cab and then load her few possessions into it. And finally Raquel Polanski was on her way to the famed *Hawke* building. She drank in the entire view of the city as she rode in the back of the cab. Skyscrapers cast gigantic shadows, occasionally spliced by the sun, slyly peeping between buildings. The windows glistened with the sun's reflection upon endless rows, each one housing the lives of a few out of a million men and women. The air remained a dark gray, corrupted by the amount of smog that polluted the air. A million different sounds of traffic rose towards heaven in a grotesque urban cacophony. She was awe-struck…in not quite the positive way. *So this is the city where dreams come true…*Raquel suddenly found that the entire scene had become monotonous and she promptly fell asleep…

After the forty-five minute drive, the driver pulled up to a strangely depressingly-colored building amidst all the shiny skyscrapers.

"Ironwood Press headqwarters." The taxi driver brought the cab to a stop." "Dat'll be fifty bucks ma'am." Raquel quickly reached into her pocket at retrieved a wad of cash that she handed to him.

"Thanks. You can keep the change."

"Oh thank ya, ma'am. Good luck to ya."

Raquel got out of the cab and watched as it took off. She stood in front of the massive concrete slab that stood towering over her. This was her future, where she belonged, no question about it! But Raquel couldn't help but feel a little apprehensive about meeting the CEO, Mr. Mitchell Schuler.

Raquel entered into the glamorous lobby. The walls shimmered with reflections of the sun creeping in. A reception desk sat in the very middle of everything. Raquel approached the front desk where a young girl busily typed away on the computer.

"Hi there, can I help you?" The receptionist smiled cheerfully.

"Yes, my name's Raquel Polanski. I believe I had an appointment with Mr. Schuler."

"Oh yes, just a moment." The young girl picked up a phone the desk and began to dial something. Raquel was still trying to take in the breathtaking display of the lobby itself. She soon found herself studying the shiny name plate that sat on the desk: **Carlin Lance**. After a minute of conversation the cheery secretary looked at her and said, "They're ready for you. Just take the elevators over there and head to floor 10. You should walk all the way to the end of the hall and encounter a big door with: **Mitchell Schuler** written across it. You can't miss it."

Raquel quickly thanked her and strode away to the elevator. The tenth story (also the topmost floor) housed the office of Mitchell Schuler which included its own waiting room and receptionist to go with it. And that was where Raquel had ended up. No matter what she tried, Raquel continued to anxiously tap her foot in anticipation for her meeting with Mr. Schuler; from what she could tell, she was the only person, besides the receptionist, who was in the vicinity of Mr. Schuler's office.

After what had seemed an eternity, the receptionist looked over at Raquel and said,

"He's ready fer ya naw, honey. But first I need to lay down the rules a' talkin' to Mr. Schuler." She beckoned Raquel over with a finger and began, "First off, ya'll find that Mr. Schuler really likes to smoke, but *do nawt* mention the smell. Secondly, ya'll only address him as 'sir' or 'Mr. Schuler' or 'the greatest CEO alive'. Is that understood?"

Raquel gave a nervous, little nod.

"Alrighty, go right ahead."

*   *   *

Ch. 3

From: christianarizonah@gmail.com

To: crzyrqlgrl@aol.com

January 1, 2014, 9:48 AM

Dear Raquel, How long has it been since we've last seen each other? Probably not since high school and that pretty nasty breakup. I'll admit that I really still miss you to this day and that's kind of the reason I'm writing this. You see, I got this really big shock to my system when I heard you were in town. I'm actually a janitor right now at Ironwood Press (sound familiar?) and just the other day I'd heard this rumor going around that this girl named Raquel Polanski who just showed up at the offices. And I think, "Wait, as in my ex, Raquel Polanski?" and sure enough it proved true. I did a little digging around and found your email (not trying to be a creeper) and thought I'd try to get in touch with you. I was wondering if we could meet up tonight, just to catch up with each other. I was wondering if around six at the Hawke building this evening if that works for you? Hopefully I'll see you there.

Love,

Christian Huck

*   *   *

The Speech Pt. I

Schuler was a heavy-set man somewhere in his mid-forties with salt-and-pepper hair that was neatly combed and partially greased to make it shine. He dressed nicely; probably picked out suits with precision and judgment. Schuler was a man of fine tastes. Everything about him screamed high-end. Even the cigar that sat just between perfectly, manicured fingers let off a bluish smoke that slowly enveloped the entire office in its suffocating fumes.

His back was turned to the door and he was slowly studying the expanse of New York City buildings that shown directly outside his office window. Mr. Schuler remained completely silent; on his desk laid the copy of Raquel's manuscript *The First Son*. After a minute he finally began to speak, "Please take a seat in front of my desk Ms. Polanski."

The voice was cold, reserved, and not at all welcoming.

"Oh, yes sir." Raquel did as she was told and quickly sat down to watch the distant CEO, continue to stare out the window.

He took a small puff of the cigar before speaking, "Ms. Polanski, do excuse me if I appear rather distant at the moment. I want to personally thank you for coming all this way to New York City. I understand this was no small journey for you."

Raquel began to pour out a nervous rush of words, "Sir, I had no problem. Really, it wasn't so much of a big deal…"

Schuler held up a hand to silence her. "No, Ms. Polanski you've come all this way and I want to tell you, your efforts were not in vain." He was still facing the window. "You've produced one of the damn best manuscripts I've ever seen at this company; a feat that is most remarkable considering your age."

Raquel could feel herself getting giddy, waiting for the moment when Schuler said, 'Welcome to Ironwood Press, Ms. Polanski!'

"And while *The First Son* was an immense pleasure to read, I found that there was something…problematical about it."

Raquel was shocked. "Excuse me sir. But would you mind telling me what exactly was wrong with it?"

Schuler only sighed a little and for the first time, turned to face her. The cigar was still smoldering. "Ms. Polanski, you're a truly great writer, you really are, and you'd make a valuable asset to this company. Now what I'm going to say hardly has to do with you, more so than it has to do with the American population at large to which one must market such novels as your own."

"You see, within the last century, mankind has encountered the single most revolutionary invention known as the television. The boob-tube, the idiot box, the one thing which brings us together; that little machine which constantly bombards one with advertisements, fads, the need to 'fit in' as we say. Well Ms. Polanski you probably wonder what the television has to do with books, well the answer my dear is: that it is quite a large amount. We are slowly desensitizing ourselves Ms. Polanski, as if we're slowly numbing ourselves to things that once entertained us. We no longer crave romance, we want erotica. We no longer desire to read of the battles fought nobly between kings, we crave to read of some sadistic serial killer ravishing some poor girl and then slowly dissemble her body in his mother's basement."

"We've become a decrepit society, Ms. Polanski. However one has to make a living and if one such you or myself wish to maintain a good life, we the 'entertainers' must cater to the wishes of such a society. The modern reader wants less and less to be *challenged* by a book than he is to be *stimulated* by it. He simply wants to find the television replicated wherever he goes, including his literature."

"The fact of the matter is, while *The First Son*, is brilliantly written, it lacks the 'televised' feel of a book. There is not nearly enough sex or violence in the book to fascinate the reader. And then to top that, you actually go off on some rather silly philosophical tangents that challenge the reader to possibly *think*. Such things only arouse emotional distress in a consumer."

Raquel could feel herself shake with rage. "Excuse me sir, but I don't agree with what you just said."

"Oh you don't? My dear, I believe you are hardly in a position to judge the issue. But, none the less, everyone is entitled to an opinion so do tell, what do *you* believe Ms. Polanski?"

The room seemed to become too small, the smoke began to give Raquel a small headache but she still managed to speak. "Sir, you and I both know there have books that have come from this company that have not met the standards you've just set."

"True, true, there have been the occasional novels that astound me and become bestsellers. Give it another fifty years Ms. Polanski and watch these kinds of novels become forgotten. Soon we shall see every bookshelf stuffed with the same cookie cutter, trashy thrillers one finds at the grocery store. And they'll each rake in the same amount of money."

Schuler began to walk around the desk and clasped a large hand on Raquel's shoulder, "That is why I need just a little bit more revision on *The First Son* and then your book will be perfectly marketable." He smiled lightly. "I'm sorry Ms. Polanski if this is not what you had in mind, but it's just the way things are. Nobody can change that."

Raquel wanted to say something more, to refute Schuler's claims. She couldn't believe that people were truly just seeking empty fascinations. "Mr. Schuler, you can't really believe that's all that people want; a cheap thrill? Surely they must crave something more. I mean as humans don't we desire something more than pleasure, something so more powerful than our cravings? Don't you believe that there are a few people out there that want something greater than pleasure in their lives? People like that have to still exist, right?"

He shrugged, "I suppose there are still quite a few who do. However, as humans, we want to live the easiest life possible. We want to receive something, without ever having to give something in return."

*　　*　　*

Ch. 4

"MY GOD MISS POLANSKI! What did it say!?" Christian stared intently at Raquel awaiting an answer.

*No, not **Him**. He couldn't have possibly shown up in my life right now. Where and how? Why did we have to come together again? Why him? Why now? Why in this place…*

"MISS POLANSKI!" Raquel was suddenly brought back down to earth by Christian's shouting. "You look as if you'd seen a ghost. Please inform me as to the contents of the email. I must know."

"It was…someone from my past." Raquel was so shocked. She hadn't expected this to happen to her right now, not in the middle of New York City. Not while trying to create a new life. *No, no, please God, no…*

"I take it from your countenance that whoever they are, they had quite an impact on your life."

She remained silent.

More than you would know.

"Some relative who disowned you, an angry ex-boss who has put a hit on you, an old friend you haven't heard from in years. Perhaps…a former lover?"

He said the last words with a delicate innocence.

"Yes."

"Did he hurt you in some way?"

That was a funny question to be asking. "No. I hurt *him*." *What was the last thing you'd said? Something really nasty probably. Something intended to wound him as much as possible. Intended to make him stay away forever…*

"What exactly did he say in the email?"

"He wanted to meet, tonight, by the *Hawke* building."

Raquel sat there; she didn't know what to feel. Receiving an email from Christian brought back feelings she never wanted to deal with again. A heart needed only to be broken once.

"Oh dear," Christian had started to look concerned for Raquel. "I believe you are in need of a true breakfast. May I invite you over for a nice repast Miss Polanski?"

She couldn't think straight, "Yes." was all she could manage. Christian slowly pushed away from the table and proceeded to help Raquel up. They left the coffee shop without another word.

They arrived at Christian's apartment a little after eleven o'clock. Most of the party goers had left except for a young woman who sat on the couch and watched a television show centered on a zombie apocalypse, filled with plenty of violence.

"Miss Polanski, I must introduce to my dear friend Miss Margaret O'Neil, a member of the Miscellaneous Department such as myself. Miss O'Neil is a connoisseur of Young Adult fiction, she's even written a little bit of her own."

The two women shook hands but said very little else. Raquel didn't want to seem completely anti-social so she posed a small question, "And what do you like about being a writer?"

"Well I think I just really love writing for younger people. I mean everyone tends to treat teens like they're more stupid than everybody else, when, I really do believe they are some of the smartest people around. They're just a lot more scared. After all it is the wildest time in a person's life. You lose your innocence, you experience new things, you learn to think for yourself, you fall in love, and you probably even have your heart broken. I really think such experiences tend to scare us. It is during times like these that we must face those questions that take us deep down, like 'what the hell does it mean to be human'? And of course there are plenty of other things to do. You can party, or do drugs, or engage in sexual behavior and forget about those questions. And then one day we'll just grow up into adults without ever having…"

Margaret's voice continued on in the background. Raquel was too heartbroken to consider the depth of her speech. *Oh man, she is chatty…*

"Why thank you Margaret," Christian had interrupted the speech. " But I do believe that poor Miss Polanski here is not entirely in the mood for such philosophical insights." Christian

42

smiled warily at Margaret who immediately began to get up from the coach.

"Actually, I kinda have to go anyway." Margaret slipped on a coat that lie near the door and became to walk out.

"Oh, I didn't mean to hasten your leave, Margaret." Christian was suddenly trying to stop his friend.

"Oh no, really Christian, I have places to go right now anyways and your poor friend does look really tired. Take good care of her okay? Have a Happy New Year's!"

Christian only nodded his head and allowed for Margaret to make her way out the door. She gave a quick smile to Raquel and Christian and then left. She'd left the T.V. on and at that moment a young muscular hero shot an arrow right into the head of an approaching zombie. Of course, there was blood.

*   *   *

The Speech Pt. II

Schuler slowly walked back to his chair and sat down with a kind of grace. There was still an eerie smile about his face. Raquel started to feel claustrophobic, like she now dreaded the very space of the office; the cigar smoke that filled the air, the light filtering in from the giant window, and the man who sat straight across from her.

"I take it that my speech has upset you quite a bit." Schuler smiled wryly and took another puff of the cigar.

"Mr. Schuler, with all due respect I'm not sure that I feel comfortable here anymore."

"Oh well." He shrugged. "However, Ironwood Press is where you're going to make a name for yourself. Considering this is your first novel I would say that I'm being rather gracious." He smiled, "I don't believe you will find an offer like this anywhere else Ms. Polanski."

Raquel smiled slightly, "I'm afraid I'll have to be leaving now." She began to push her chair back when Schuler started to speak again.

"But to be fair to you, I must give you a taste of what life is like here at Ironwood Press.

Besides you'll never know what you missed out on."

Raquel hesitated. She wanted to be published, but was Ironwood Press really where she wanted to do that? *Was it really worth it?* She sat herself back down. "How do you run things at Ironwood Press, Mr. Schuler?"

Again he stood up, stretched his legs and commenced on some lengthy speech. "Here at Ironwood Press we find that organization is rather necessary in order for one to maintain a well-run company. The building itself is divided into several 'departments'. " He paused and smiled, "Each 'department' is solely dedicated to a specific genre of literature. So naturally they consist of writer's who all act, think, speak, and resemble one another. I mean everyone's much more comfortable if they are placed with people who are just like themselves. It's easier for them to associate with those kinds of people." He set down his cigar and started to pace in front of the giant window. "Most people, Ms. Polanski, are not comfortable being around those who are *different*. People are more comfortable with what they know and are familiar with. Everything else is, foreign, alien, and unlikeable." The cigar slowly sizzled in a glass ashtray; the once bright red tip had become a dull orange. Schuler finally took a seat. "It was under my initiative that the company was reformed. I saw that people worked more efficiently if you placed them in homogenous groups. They worked better and more efficiently, which in turn, made more money for the company."

"For example," Schuler reached into a drawer within his desk and retrieved a laminated piece of paper. "We have plenty of departments here; one to suit every kind of writer and his or her interests." He slid the paper across to Raquel, who was amazed by the number of departments listed on the paper. It reminded her of all those circles in Dante's *Inferno*.

"Cream-of-the-Crop" Department

Entertainment Department

Social Department

PUBLIC RELATIONS DEPARTMENT

Theatre Department

HOW-TO DEPARTMENT

Erotica Department

BURN OUT DEPARTMENT

Miscellaneous Department

Miscellaneous Department, thought Raquel. *Who the hell belongs to the Miscellaneous Department?* Schuler continued on with his speech, "It's always in due time that new writers such as yourself should…for lack of a better word, *conform* to one of these departments. I should say assimilate into a group identity."

Raquel did not like Schuler's choice of wording. "Um, what if I'm not so willing to do that?"

He only grimaced. "When writers prove to be troublesome and refuse to identify with one of the departments, to take on the personalities exhibited within that department, they are either immediately dismissed from Ironwood Press," Schuler paused. "Or…they are put into that dreadful Miscellaneous Department."

"What's that?"

"Only the most god-awful idea this company has ever had." He began to massage his temples as if he was suddenly besieged by a heaven-sent headache. "When I began the departments, some writers had rebelled against the idea. They didn't want to assume an identity, to become a part of something greater than themselves. They refused to, if you will, 'hop on the bandwagon'." He was slowly crushing the last remains of the cigar in the tray.

"So what's the problem with this department? Do they cause a lot of trouble?"

Schuler only moaned, "OHHH! All they do is cause trouble! I must say that there is nothing worse in our company than that stupid department, aside from maybe that program we instated for the burn-outs; nothing but a waste of company money and time. The Miscellaneous Department is a sort of last resort for many writers. Most of them leave the company altogether within a few months."

"Granted, we do have a few authors, such as Christian Martinez, who can still generate plenty of income for the company. However, most of those writers are those who are not evolving with society. They forget for whom they write. They are selfish and they shall die out one day. No one will ever remember who Joyce, Kerouac, Vonnegut, or Dickens were, much less Christian Martinez." There was a frighteningly wide smile across Schuler's face which repulsed Raquel. She had begun to tense up in the chair, but it must have shown. "I see I've possibly frightened you. I'm very sorry but you must remember that I am the one who runs this company and I will see to it that everyone and everything is in their natural place. You see Miss Polanski, it may seem bad to belong to a group but in fact it helps us to establish who we are and what we believe in and if you would just give this a chance you can find that it's a very beautiful thing. When we become part of something, be it a club, religion, a clique, or whatever, we also learn to adopt a certain label that comes attached to that group. That label serves to establish who we are to everyone else. And that damn Miscellaneous Department doesn't have sense enough to accept that. They don't want a label; they feel as if it 'encases them in a stereotype' to put it in their own words." Schuler put on a paternal smile now and leaned across his desk to get closer to Raquel.

"None of these accusations are true Ms. Polanski; it is in a fact a thing a thing of beauty and identity."

Raquel had had quite enough of his speech. She pushed back the chair, stood up, and briskly paced herself to the door.

"Just remember, you will *never* have an opportunity like this again!" Schuler had raised his voice. "You think your chances of being published somewhere else are higher? Ha! Good luck with that!"

She was stung. Raquel wretched open the door before she heard his voice call out again. "Why turn down this offer? Hell, I'm practically guaranteeing you a job. I can make you famous Raquel, and rich. Good writers like you hardly come around but when they do, oh, do they make bank."

Raquel found herself frozen in her tracks. Riches and fame appealed to anyone's mind with young ears, even Raquel's. "Please," coaxed Schuler, "just close the door, come right back in, and me and you will have a little chat."

She inexplicably obeyed, maybe out of desire, maybe out of fear. Raquel turned around to face the dreaded CEO. Raquel yearned for fame and money, but was it worth the price? She was persuaded otherwise.

"Okay. What do you want me to do?"

*   *   *

Christian had attempted to make scrambled eggs for both him and Raquel. Neither really ate, partially because their consciousnesses were clouded and because the eggs were the same quality as those found at most chain-restaurants. He had also attempted to engage Raquel in some small talk but she didn't open up very much.

"Miss Polanski, what if we decided to take a stroll? I do believe meandering in the fresh air can purify one's conscious. I know a particularly wonderful park just nearby. The weather may be not ideal for walking but the park is just magnificent." Raquel didn't protest; if Christian said it was bound to do something good, the walk probably would.

"And how did you make your way to Ironwood Press?" Raquel could see her breath as the question escaped out into the open air. She and Christian were walking in the little park; park benches were covered in snow, and the trees stretched out there cold, naked limbs, waiting for spring to return and awaken them once again.

"I was always an eccentric, young fellow. Always day dreaming, had my head in the clouds. Psychoanalysists would blame it on my parents. They were always reading me some fantastic fairy tale with anthropomorphic pigs that maintained a work ethic, or damsels in distress that were rescued by some knight in shining armor. And then came school and I did horribly at mathematics and most of the sciences. I never did have a mind for the absolute. I desired the abstract. Such was my entire life in school. I was raised in one of those small picturesque towns, where everybody goes about knowing each other's deepest, darkest secrets. It doesn't surprise one that I had met and fallen in love with a girl, Sonya. We were both in our last year of high school and had known each other our entire lives. It was only natural that we suddenly fell madly in love."

"So we were young, in love, hormone-ridden; in essence: we were idiots. After graduating we decided to elope, which we did, much to our parents' dismay. To top that off we were both writers. We desired fame, to be able to walk into a bookstore and see *our* books taking up space on the shelves. So, we decided to head for New York City, of all places. We were poor but, that did not matter. Remember, we were in love. To support our small apartment we both had to work day jobs. I found work in a used bookstore run by a Mr. Harrison, a British immigrant, who, God bless him, treated me like a son. Sonya found work at a Hebrew grocery store where she slaved away. Then we would both come home in the evenings, exhausted, brow-beaten, a bit jaded, and yet we still had time for our novels and each other. Heaven knows where we got the time to be intimate."

Christian slightly blushed at this comment. Raquel only giggled a little, "Go on…"

"We, as you must know, desired to have children. We made several attempts, yet nothing occurred. Then it was on one dark and snowy January day, I remember it well, we made our way to the obstetrician. He commenced testing my wife and the verdict: she was barren. Adoption would never be an option given our financial situation. Our hopes of ever having a family ended right there. And that's when things began to deteriorate."

"We came home, Sonya and I, and all she did was cry. I held her for a while before she had cried herself to sleep and then I snuck out. I was angry, heartbroken, confused, and I had no intention of ending up at a bar, but somehow I made my way there. At the bar I ordered some hard liquor but I can't recall why I did so. I was never a drinker in high school; I was always the teetotaler during parties, but that night I ordered some very hard liquor and consumed every last ounce. After that, my drinking gradually progressed. I snuck out night after night trying to find solace in a cup by drowning my sorrows. My dipsomania progressed from secrecy to a sordid candidness. I would stagger into the apartment in the evenings and she would smell it on me. Sonya would see my haggard face, my sunken eyes and say, 'Baby, you need help.' I even remember how she would do it, too. Sonya would brace her arm around my back and move it in a circular fashion, as if trying to soothe a lost child. You see, she knew I had lost my job; Mr. Harrison died and his son took over the business. Harrison Jr. had no intention of employing a dipsomaniac, so I was fired. I went home and cradled whiskey bottles to my chest as I scribbled out incoherent balderdash on paper. All that I produced within that time was garbage."

"Sonya would come home and try to soothe me. She put up with all my nonsense." Christian suddenly stopped. Raquel studied his face only to find that his eyes had watered over. "Raquel, Sonya lived with a monster at that time, not a man. But she stilled loved him. I played the part in our little doomed love affair and then things finally snapped. I eventually hit her." Now Raquel could really hear the quaver in his voice. "It was only once but I had no such intention to inflict pain on my little Sonya. It was a rainy cold night in March, of course I had been out of the house completely consuming drink upon drink upon drink and arrived home inebriated. Sonya approached me and told me she was leaving me; that she loved me so much that she had to leave me; that I needed help. In my stupidity I started to protest and bar her way when she reached out to pull my hand away and I struck her. It was on her cheek, the right one. Afterwards she looked horrified, like she had come face-to-face with a monster. I was ashamed and disgusted with myself. She pushed passed me, carrying nothing but her suitcase filled with clothes and her personal manuscript. I watched as she disappeared down the hall and down the stair landing. In that moment I decided to get outrageously intoxicated. I began at about eight o'clock that night and did not stop for about forty five minutes before I felt incredibly nauseous. The vomiting did not cease until I had finally fainted in my own pool of bile and alcohol."

"By some miracle I had forgotten to close the door after Sonya's flight and my next door neighbor had become concerned when he first heard the retching from through the wall. He snuck over, like any good neighbor and peeped through the door only to stumble upon me in my miserable condition. He called emergency services and saw to my recovery in the hospital. But like a good neighbor he was rather nosey and raided my apartment. My neighbor was, and still is a literary agent at Ironwood Press. At the time, he discovered my manuscript that I'd written in drunken stupor. A two hundred page mess of a doomed love affair (much alike my own) which followed narratives from both sides of the story. The girl, Danielle (pet named: Dani) was in a tumultuous affair with her lover Ian, but alas such a love affair could not last. Ian fell to alcoholism and Dani had to make up for Ian's slothfulness with her hard work. Then, climatically, they both died in a car accident. It was utter garbage like I said and yet my neighbor, a Mr. Colin Williams, presented the manuscript to Mr. Schuler and passed it off as 'postmodernism'. I stayed in the hospital to fix my very unstable kidneys and liver before I heard of the proposal from Ironwood Press to publish my novel and to offer me a position in the offices. I cannot say why I allowed it at the time; perhaps because I desperately needed money. Anyways the book was finally published, people loved it. Critics applauded the novel's 'emotional charge'. Yet no one knew, not a single soul knew that what they had read actually happened."

Raquel couldn't believe it. They had both completely stopped walking; Christian had his eyes veered towards the ground. "Christian, I am so sorry…"

"Don't be Miss Polanski. The past has come and gone. There is nothing we can do to change it."

They walked on a little further. *Apparently that was a really loaded question.* Raquel was still wondering if she had pried too deep.

"So what became of your book, I mean, I never heard of it…"

"My book," Christian let a slight sigh of misty breathe into the air, "it was titled *This Love* and I had that damned book run out of print."

Raquel only nodded sympathetically, "I can see why."

"Yes, I have no desire to continue with those dreadful memories again. I've had my fair share of traumatic experiences and I have no intention of turning to them again." He smiled warily and they both continued walking along the paved path before someone spoke again.

"And what about you Miss Polanski, you must have some story of how you came to Ironwood Press as well."

So she told him.

*   *   *

Virgil Everley/Nausea

Schuler answered in a calm voice, "We here at Ironwood Press would love for you to get a sense of what it's like here. So I'm going to treat to you to a complimentary tour of our company headquarters."

Raquel nodded slightly. "Is that all…"

"Of course!" Schuler laughed, "At least give it a chance. I should think you'd find that Ironwood Press is truly an amazing workplace. I'll have one of the interns escort you around."

Schuler pressed a small button on the office phone and started to speak into it, "Lydia, please ring up the intern Mr. Everley, ASAP. I would like for him to give a tour of the *Hawke* building to Ms. Polanski."

"Yes sir." was the short, monotone reply.

"You will thoroughly enjoy the tour, Ms. Polanski." Schuler smiled as he hung up the phone.

Raquel gave up. She figured that there could not be any real damage done by the tour.

Not even a minute had passed when a young man stepped into the office. He had straight, neatly combed blonde hair and a smile that revealed a mouthful of pristine, pearl-colored teeth; a smile that was absolutely priceless. Raquel thought to herself that he must be the

60

tour guide; not that she wouldn't mind letting a possibly single and very good looking young man be her's.

"Mr. Schuler, you wanted to see me?" The young man inquired.

"Yes indeed. Mr. Everley this is Raquel Polanski. Ms. Polanski this is one of our interns, Virgil Everley."

They both shook hands briefly and exchanged a few words. "It's a pleasure to meet you Mr. Everley." Raquel politely nodded.

"Please, just call me Virgil."

She blushed at his proposal.

"Now Mr. Everley," Schuler began, "I want you to give Raquel a full tour of the premises starting from the top of the building and working your way down to the last floor." He paused. "I trust that Ms. Polanski will be in good hands despite your being rather young and therefore inexperienced. Is that correct Mr. Everley?"

"Yes sir." The young man answered quickly.

"Well that's settled. Now Ms. Polanski," he faced Raquel. "If you won't mind, I would like to keep you manuscript in my office for the day and I will make sure that you are able to pick it up by tomorrow at the latest, if that would be all right with you?"

Raquel hesitated; she wasn't so sure she wanted to leave her work in the hands of a man like Schuler. There was no telling what he could do.

"If you don't mind Mr. Schuler, I would prefer to pick it up at the end of the day."

He only shrugged. "Fine, I can arrange that. Just remember to stop by. Now Mr. Everley if you wouldn't mind, I think Ms. Polanski is still waiting patiently for her tour. I trust she's in good hands and please remember: you may observe everything but be sure to disturb _**nothing**_."

"Yes sir. Miss Polanski and I will make sure to do just that." He motioned to Raquel for her to follow him.

As they left through the door Schuler cried out, "Don't forget my offer Ms. Polanski. One just like it may never appear!" And with that, Raquel left the offices she had in fact dreaded the whole time.

Schuler waited for the door to be completely closed. He stared at the manuscript on his desk and started to feel extremely nauseous.

*   *   *

\

Raquel's story was not as nearly as fantastical as Christian's but she did have a story, nonetheless. Both of them continued shuffling their feet against the snow as they made their way to some unknown destination. Raquel was the first to speak. "I've got a friend, Sarah, she wanted to meet me today but I was so exhausted I didn't even bother to send a reply. Do you mind if we took a detour to her little café? I swear it won't take that long."

Christian nodded in exasperated agreement, "I don't see any harm. We've both had a dismal morning; I don't see why an early lunch won't upset anything."

So they consented and made their way to *Sarah's* gourmet bakery, not but a few blocks away. Upon arriving in the bakery, Raquel found herself greeted by a friend she hadn't seen in years. In fact, she had not seen Sarah since high school.

"Come on in! Please make yourselves comfortable, I'll be with you in just a moment." Christian had wandered off to admire some baked goods. Sarah was spoiling her two guests while hastily trying to undo her flour-coated apron and fixing her hair that had been tied in a neat bun. Sarah had hardly changed after so many years. She still retained that seemingly endless smile and the same bespectacled face that always seemed so warm and caring.

The two caught up with each other, their career choices, who they still kept in touch with, and especially what had brought them to New York City. Sarah had always had a passion for baking, something she took advantage of in high school, constantly bringing home-made goods to her friends at school. They both laughed over certain football games, different dances, the various friends they had had...

"Do you stay in touch with all of them?" Sarah had posed the question.

"Not really. There weren't a lot of people I stayed in touch with after high school."

Sarah stayed quiet for a second. "Did you ever regret not staying in touch with them?"

"Who, people in high school?"

"Well somewhat, I figured that we just...ya know, stopped talking."

"But doesn't that make you sad? I mean, having a relationship like that and just cutting it off."

Raquel shrugged. "People come and go, we all change…"

"Yeah but did you ever wonder why you could stop so easily? Was something ever worth it if you gave it up so easily?"

They both remained silent for awhile after Sarah's comment. Raquel finally broke the silence, "Well, high school's a funny time for everyone…"

"Yeah, it is. But think about how foolish we all were then. Trying to lose our innocence as quickly as possible, talking as if we knew it all, dressing however we needed to, all in order to be in the *in crowd*." Sarah paused. "And to think how much it actually mattered in the end. I mean for God's sake look at us. You're an aspiring author come to New York and I'm a successful businesswoman. How much did all *that* in high school really matter? I wish we hadn't treated it like it was the most important thing in our lives."

It was a long time after that that either of them spoke again. Sarah took a quick glance at a wristwatch before standing up to go. "Well, it's about time to get back to work. Thanks for stopping by." Raquel stood up to give her a great big hug. "Hey, good luck on your book." Sarah softly whispered in her ear before retracting and making her way back to the kitchen. Raquel only smiled and began to exit the bakery before she caught a glimpse of Christian trying to wave her down. "Miss Polanski," he yelled, "Do come over here! I must introduced you to Mr. Williams!" Christian was sitting at a corner table with a rather tall, lanky individual who sat with his legs crossed and a cigarette protruding from his hand.

Christian motioned her over so she obeyed and took a seat next to the two gentlemen.

"Miss Polanski, this is my agent, Colin Williams."

*   *   *

A Violent Memory

Mitchell Schuler was kneeling on the bathroom floor, his knees bent as if he was praying to the porcelain god before him. "Keep a watch on all incoming calls; tell everybody I'll be back in a few minutes. I need to use the restroom." He had told his secretary moments before quickly leaving the room, not a moment after Virgil and Raquel had left the office. He was now bowing before the toilet; his head hovering just inches above the bowl. The entire room was spinning…*Good god, that girl couldn't have known, nobody knows goddamnit! Your secret is safe; how the hell is some girl from across the country going to know about it? But something about that book*…Prince Adam watched as the approaching rays of dawn illuminated the splotches of blood…The retching began and Schuler found his body began to violently curl itself around the toilet seat…*The First Son! It's like she was there*… **"How about me and you head inside and get more of that champagne?" Schuler smiled. Mr. Benjamin was standing on the patio outside of the room…**that stained the tips of his fingers. It had been an extremely difficult task, killing the old king…but the first heave proved to be a dry one. The second one was not as kind…*watching me and him, and the whole thing. She couldn't have. Nobody was.*

68

Nobody did. You damn fool… **"Just pour me a glass and bring it out here." Mr. Benjamin was studying the stars**…Of course the old fool had been sound asleep. He hadn't brought any wenches to bed that night. "My luck." thought the prince…bits of what appeared to be breakfast now sloshed in the bowl…*if you allow this to control you, it will only destroy you…***while Schuler walked over to the champagne bottle. Instead of pouring any he began to slowly loosen his tie**…He had crept into the room right around midnight and watched for some time as the moonlight blanketed the sleeping king…The third retch brought up the remainder of eggs Benedict, which had been subsequently followed with coffee…*You're paranoid. See. It's already destroying your insides*…**it was some expensive, silk tie, some Christmas gift no doubt**…The prince unsheathed his sword and greedily began to gaze upon it…The bile stung his throat. The retching had become so violent that tears poured from his eyes…*good god! Someone make it stop! It's killing me! It's* *killing me...***and now it would have other purposes***...The throne was only a quick thrust away...A fourth retch resulted in a generous outpour of indigested cereal bits into the bowl...*Is that the Frosty Flakes...*"However I choose to," the prince thought to himself, "I must do it quickly and be careful not to get the blood everywhere."...**He now had the tie completely off. Schuler wrapped it around his own neck to get an approximate measure**...Schuler's hand shakily reached for the lever...*oh god*...Adam slowly raised his sword... **"I really do enjoy working with you." Schuler was slowly encroaching upon Mr. Benjamin who, still had his back turned towards the ship and was unaware of his colleague**...and quickly pulled down, hoping to wash the vomit smell away...*My plan was perfect*...to sink it into the king's soft body...**"But you know," Schuler was standing on the deck besides Mr. Benjamin, "there** could be a little change that could take place."

"Well, if it's all the same to you Mitch what change did you have a min..."...There was another dry retch...*I've got nothing left in my stomach*...Before he could drive the deadly blade home the King's eyes opened, contorted in a look of fear and shock...**Schuler had brought the tie-turned-noose around Mr. Benjamin's neck and began to pull furiously**...and then all the convulsions stopped...*I think that's the worst of it*...The king just as quickly deflected the blow with a sword that he kept by his side in bed...**Mr. Benjamin's initial reaction was more than expected if not comically cliché; his hands began grasping for the neck, desperately trying to tear the tie off**...Schuler was laying across the tile floor...*thank god it stopped*...Prince Adam was taken aback by the old king's swiftness, but did not allow that to stop him. Using his foot he quickly delivered a kick into

71

the old man's head…**Schuler kept his grab tight and listened to the horrible sounds of his boss gasping for a gulp of air. With one swift motion Mr. Benjamin had forced the two men onto the ground. He began to kick his legs in a futile attempt to break free. The strangler and strangled were moving in a circular path**…As if from an unexpected crevice, the sickness began again and a stream of vomit began to creep up his throat and into his mouth. It spewed across the bathroom floor…*I'm choking!*…There was a cry of pain and the king released his grip from the sword. It fell to the earth with a clang. Prince Adam drove his sword home…**Mr. Benjamin began to flop about now and Schuler only pulled tighter. It only took a minute before the convulsions began to slow down**…Schuler tried to prop himself up on the toilet before the vomit got anywhere else…*heavy breathing*…The sword nestled itself just beneath the king's ribs. Prince Adam smiled as the blade sunk farther and farther in and a red stain began to form on the king's white night gown...**the kicking suddenly came to a stop. Schuler looked over at the body. Mr. Benjamin's eyes were rolled up and his face had become a strange hue of purple**...Another dry heave and Schuler smashed his face into the edge of the seat...The king's body fell limp to the ground. His eyes had turned up white and a small trickle of blood seeped from the mouth...**Schuler could see the whites of Mr. Benjamin's eyes; a small stream of blood dripped from the mouth**...Schuler had caused part of his mouth to bleed on account of the facial collision with the porcelain..._I need to get this cleaned up before anyone sees anything_...Prince Adam now stood, gloating over the body of his fallen father. He quickly disposed of the body by pushing it from the window into the moat. A sword was driven through him to make it appear a suicide. But now the task was complete and the throne was all his...**The body was disposed of quickly; a quick tip over the edge of the boat and Mr.**

Benjamin disappeared into the murky water of Upper New York Bay. All the others on the top of the yacht would be partying too loud to hear anything. But Schuler had finished what he needed to do and Ironwood Press, was now all his...It took a full twenty minutes before Schuler had wiped up the vomit around the stall and had cleaned his mouth. He stood at the mirror tending to his bleeding teeth...*Nothing chipped, thank god*...and trying to wipe a dried piece of vomit that sat at the corner of mouth. Schuler quickly tidied up his suit, fixed his hair, and quickly rinsed with mouthwash. For a moment, he continued to stare back at his reflection in the mirror...*It's amazing how corrupt a person could be and you wouldn't even know it. Your best friend, your neighbor, a relative, the mailman, each one of them could be hiding some deep dark secret and you'd never even guess it. That's what being guilty does to you. It implodes in you. Guilt feeds off of your emotions like a parasite. It turns you cynical and soon you believe that everyone else is just like you. A monster; harboring some deep dark secret of the soul*...before he made a disastrous conclusion…*Nobody should ever mess with dark truths, or violent memories. For those who do, there is a hell of a price to pay, Ms. Polanski.*

*   *   *

Ch. 7

Colin Williams was a younger gentleman of rather pale complexion and Oscar Wilde-esque hair which slowly curled past a certain length. Colin was so tall that he seemed large even sitting down. Christian had just introduced Raquel to him and Mr. Williams did not hesitate to offer a warm handshake.

'It sure's nice to meet you Raquel."

"I'm happy to meet you too Mr. Williams…"

"Just call me Colin, I'm not much for formalities."

Raquel just smiled a little. He was strange person, Colin; vastly eccentric.

"So Christian tells me you're looking to get published at IP right now"

"Yeah, I've just got this manuscript I'm trying to get published right now. It's called *The First Son*. Nothing to brag about much, just a thriller set in middle-ages England…"

"Hey that's still awesome. I dig that idea."

Christian suddenly interrupted, "I'm sorry to cut in but, Miss Polanski, I must tell you that Mr. Williams here is my personal agent and was the 'neighbor' who 'discovered' my literary talents."

"And how exactly did you become involved at Ironwood Press." Raquel was now intently studying Colin.

"Well it's actually a funny story. See, unlike Christian I actually *went to* and *finished* college. Only I majored in developmental psychology…"

"What does that have to do with publishing…"

"Wait, it's not just finished yet. So I had finished with this degree but I had minored in English. I wanted to practice working with children but I eventually quit after being told by the parents that my practices were 'too unusual' or 'strange'."

"What did you do?"

"Me? Oh see I thought that the way parents raised their kids was wrong. I criticized people for it and as you know, people do not take criticism well, especially in something they think they know more than you. 'Do you have children?' they'd ask. 'No.' was the obvious answer. And then they'd tell me to stop sticking my nose in places it didn't belong. You see I had trouble with using a belt or other materials to punish children. I said that they shouldn't do it and they laughed and say 'Well where's your experience with children if you don't have any of your own?' But I'd just point at their own child and say, 'I was that kid; the one who was on the receiving end of all those punishments.'"

"I had come to this conclusion that I was raised wrong. Shortly after I became sixteen I started to question my motives. It had never occurred to me until that moment why I had even done the things I did. I had simply been taught to do the 'right things'. So I systematically did things, like a robot, because it was 'the right thing'. But my heart remained empty and unchanged".

"When you were a child you always did things because your parents instilled in you some idea that if you didn't do the right thing, there'd be some horrible punishment for it. The belt, the time out chair and corner, the 'go-to-your-room!'s and 'no-dessert-for-you's served to establish this fact early on. We had to do the right thing because something bad might happen, in which case our conscience was ruled by fear and guilt. And your heart remains unchanged."

"Our parents thought they could control our hearts but the truth is no matter how old you are or even what point in your life you are in, nobody can change your heart except yourself. I wanted to see if parents could possibly raise their kids in a different way, one that didn't make the kid grow up doing things just because they were 'right'; not because it was another catechism to recite, another dogma to follow, another commandment to obey, no, I wanted kids doing things because their heart called them to do it. That they did it out of pure, unconditional, non-behavioral, love. Something that could only be done of their own free will. But I was rejected, called an 'amateur', laughed at, told that my plans were a 'delusion', and that I'd never succeed."

"So I packed my bags, hit the road and landed a job as an editor at a nascent publishing house called Ironwood Press at the time. I was an editor for everyone until that dammed

Schuler came in and created his departments!" Colin had suddenly smashed his fist down on the table. "To hell with it all!"

Raquel could feel how angry and heart-broken he was. "I'm really sorry Colin…"

Colin seemed to calm down for a second before he shrugged nonchalantly. "I suppose you can't go through life living with regrets. After all it's because of everything that I'm here right now: sitting at a table enjoying good conversation with you and Christian over some coffee." He smiled before quietly looking at his watch. A sudden anxious expression clouded his face. "I'm very sorry but I'm afraid I have to be going. I promised to help with all that crap with Gold Canyon Publishers this evening."

"You volunteered for that rubbish?" Christian had spat out the question.

"Well, I had nothing better to do this New Year's Day. I figured I'll see some peeps from the office."

He stood up quickly before taking leave of Christian and Raquel. "It was pleasure to meet you Raquel." Colin stood with arms wide open, waiting for a reciprocated hug.

"Oh, why the hell not?" Raquel found herself hugging somebody she had known for only a few minutes before he quickly left the café.

"What was he talking about when he said the stuff about a Gold Canyon Publishers?"

"I shall explain later my Miss Polanski, let us depart and find a more suitable place to talk. But if I remember there is something very interesting in the very idea that Mr. Huck should want to rendezvous with you tonight at the Hawke building."

"Why's that?"

"Because you two will be utterly alone."

*   *   *

The Call

"Sam?"

"Yeah?"

"Schiano is that you?"

"Yeah. This is Schuler ain't it?"

"Yes, yes. First I need to know: are you in a private place?"

"Yeah, of course. I'm not an idiot Schuler; I know ta take business-related calls when I'm all on my lonesome."

"Okay good, but I gotta be brief. I'm using my work phone."

"Aww fer chrissakes'; ya wanna get both our asses iced?"

"No, no, no, Sam. I just don't have time right now…"

"Golly sounds like someone's got trouble on their hands. I take it this *is* another business offer, right?"

"Yes, I just" *exhales* "I just need to take care of this one a bit differently."

"Sure thing. Give it ta me straight."

"Okay, so there's this girl, name's Raquel Polanski. She grew up in the Middle-of-Nowhere, U.S.A. and she just showed up at the offices today. I need you to get digging. Find out about her and then draw her in. You see I need you to do it differently this time."

" Alrighty, hit me already. I'm all ears."

"I want you to bring in the girl alive, to me personally."

slight pause "Okay. Wow. Never thought I'd become a bounty hunter but uhh…okay. If that's whatcha want."

"So how much?"

"I'd see, ehh, about 500G's should cut it."

"Holy shit…"

"Hey, ey, ey, times are gettin' rough Sully. I just got done with a job in Santa Fe and these punk-ass fuzzies just started ta follow me. I've seen the little bastards everywhere since then. I feel like they're tailing me…"

"Wait, does that mean this message is possibly being recorded?!"

"Aww, calm ya tits Sully, you ain't in trouble til yer caught. Right?"

"Yes. I guess so…"

"Now don't get all pissy on me. Times' hard for most people. I gotta eat and live too, ya know."

"I guess so…"

"Alrighty, well I'll begin once I get up to the Big Apple. Say is there any time and place you'd prefer to have me round her in?"

"New Year's Day in my offices; they'll be completely empty. No one will be here."

"Okay, sounds like a plan. Oh, and I'll probably be up there at about noon. I need access to yer janitors' uniforms…"

"What? Why…"

"Don't question. Just do. You wanted me to snoop around didn' ya?"

sigh"Yes."

"So, I want access to those uniforms when I get up there. Got it?"

"Yes…I suppose so…"

"Alrighty see you soon Sully. If I don't, have a Merry Christmas."

".Merry Christmas to you too Schiano."

"Oh hey wait. I really don't have any business asking about clienteles' motives but why do ya need this girl brought to ya, alive?"

inhales deep, long pause"Because I gotta do it myself. I have to be the one that pulls the trigger…"

*   *   *

"Every January," Christian and Raquel were sitting upon a park bench as he described a rivalry without an equal in all of history. "An annual competition is held much like those of the Greek theaters of yore. Every New Year's Day, Ironwood Press competes against its sister company Gold Canyon Publishers. For a whole 24 hour period, writers from both companies compete in various competitions against one another like 'Best Short Story', 'Best Poem', 'Best Pulp Fiction Short Story', 'Best Book Review', and many more. But those things are just dreadful, absolutely awful wastes of one's time."

"Why?" Raquel asked.

"Because I have never seen writers stoop so low. Cheating, booing, occasional altercations, and obscene insults tossed about rather liberally, they treat each other like they are less human and more like animals encroaching on one another's territory. Frankly I find it all rather stupid and fraught with jingoistic over-zealousness."

Raquel shook her head. "It's sad that some people allow differences to get in the way of things."

"Why you're very right Miss Polanski, in fact, I couldn't agree with you more. I feel as though that's the best thing you've said all day."

She shot him a cold glance.

"I didn't say you never said anything *good*, I simply said that that was the best."

They both laughed a little and continued to scan the park. It was still too cold for most people to come out but those who did were the few children crazy enough to go out and build snowmen. Raquel felt okay though. She was grateful to be out of the offices and out and about with some crazy author she'd met in the middle of New York City and who'd simultaneously invited her to a New Year's Party. And now they were out and about trying to find her ex-lover who may have been trying to fall in love with her again. Everything was seemingly perfect.

Suddenly Raquel noticed the outline of someone clad in a heavy overcoat making their way towards them. As the figure got closer and closer she could distinguish it was a woman and instantly she knew who she was…

"It's Valerie, Valerie Dictorian!" Raquel began to cry-out-loud. Christian turned his head in the same direction.

"Come, come now. How are you acquainted with Miss Dictorian?"

*   *   *

The Cream of the Crop Department

The tour began as simple one sided monologue in which Virgil continued to droll on and on about Ironwood Press' history.

"Ironwood Press started in the year 2001, the work and vision of one man who envisioned a company in which writers could write side by side, displaying their works in an array of…"

They hadn't gotten very far from Schuler's office, which from the reception room, emptied into a giant hallway filled with offices. Each office looked the same: a brown, wooden door with a sort of grainy looking window (the kind that are often used in shower doors to blur one's private parts) that allowed for light to filter in, while allowing the occupant to maintain some minimal privacy. On each window stenciled in, were giant letters that read: **Ironwood Press**, and underneath that, was listed whoever occupied the office and their various occupations. Raquel could tell that the occupants in this hallway were almost unanimously authors.

The hall was illuminated by a sort of softer luminescence that came from lamps that lined the top of the walls. The lamps consisted of a white cover that hid the light bulbs but allowed for the light to trickle out in a stream that resembled a haze. The walls were colored baize and had one single brown stripe that continued on until the end of the wall forced it to stop along with it. Another peculiar feature is that not another living soul could be seen all the way up and down the hall. It was perfectly silent. *It looks mature, intelligent, and perfect. I like it.* Raquel was silently observing every little thing about the place.

Virgil continued to ramble on until he reached a point in his speech and began to stutter, "…with the passing of our old CEO, Mitchell Schuler took over the company after rising from his position in the…the…" He suddenly burst out in rage. "DAMN IT! I forget!"

Raquel stood shocked. She tried to console him. "It's okay, whatever you forgot…I'm sure it can't be *that* important."

"It is though! Ever intern here is charged with the task of memorizing the company's history, word-for-word, just in case we have to give tours to incoming writers here." He looked rather upset.

"It's okay. You don't have to recite some giant pre-made speech to give a tour. Really you don't have to worry about what I think."

"Thank God! I never thought I'd meet someone who wouldn't care. Please Raquel, let's cut this crap and I'll just show you the different departments. We can go at whatever pace you want and please, feel free to ask any questions!"

"Sure thing! But uhh, where the heck are we?" She motioned to the hallway around them.

"Oh, this place? You're in the one and only C.O.T.C department."

"The what?"

"I mean The 'Cream-of-the-Crop' Department respectively. Schuler keeps all these guys locked up on the top floor along with himself. These guys are the really hard core writers, producing bestsellers that sell thousands of copies within their first week of publication!"

Wow. Raquel was in awe.

"Mhmm. And Schuler only keeps the ones who can write a novel that will sell at least $100,000 in the first week. As you can imagine these guys write novels like there's no tomorrow. And they rake in a lot of cold-hard cash for Schuler. That's why they're 'so far up' both in the company and the building."

Raquel peered at the various names written on the doors. "Can I meet one?"

"Um, sure. I guess we could peek in on someone and observe them working. Now let's see…" Virgil looked around at the various doors, like some kid in a candy store that couldn't make up his mind. "Oh yeah, I know someone you could meet."

He led Raquel to a door that read: **Valerie Dictorian- Author**. Raquel wondered who could be sitting behind the door when Virgil made a loud knocking on it.

"Go away." A groggy-sounding voice snapped from behind the door.

"Hey Valerie, I've got someone who would love to meet you!" Virgil said in his most cheery voice.

"I'm not in the mood you moron. Tell them to go bother someone else."

Virgil continued to coax. "Really Valerie, it's a huge fan and they were wondering if for just a few minutes…"

A sharp cry cut him off. "I'm not taking any damn visitors you idiot of an intern. Now screw off before I get security up here"

Raquel was shocked by the harshness exhibited by whoever Miss Dictorian was.

"Alright then Valerie; you brought this upon yourself."

"No, what the hell are you doing?! You try any funny business and I swear to God…"

In one fell swoop Virgil, acting on behalf of T.V. show detectives everywhere, had kicked the door using all the power of his right leg. The door swung open and a high-pitched shriek emerged from within the small office space.

"'THE HELL DO YOU THINK YOU'RE DOING?!"

Virgil only smirked as he entered into the office. "You didn't want to open the door. You asked for it."

Raquel stepped in right after Virgil only to be shocked by what she saw. The office was in complete disarray. Papers lay strewn about in no particular order and several book shelves had been thrown on the ground. A giant desk sat at the back of the room and the apparent origin of the irritable voice was sitting at it. The voice had belonged to a woman dressed in a sharp black dress that was completely wrinkled. Her hair was shot out in every direction as in a bad case of bed head. She looked exhausted; her eyes were bloodshot and sunken into a face that cruelly accented her idea to forget makeup and

93

lipstick for the day. A name plate on the desk in front of her revealed her to be the one and only Miss Valerie Dictorian. Alongside that was an unlabeled bottle that carried an amber-colored liquid that was more than likely alcoholic.

"I want you out of my office now!" She snapped at Virgil. "And her too!" She pointed with an uninviting finger towards Raquel.

"Aww, what's the matter Valerie?" Virgil asked.

"I don't want to talk about it." She seemed on the verge of tears.

"C'mon, you can tell me anything."

Suddenly in a fit of a rage, Valerie seized a piece of paper and hurled it with all her might at Virgil. It only fluttered to the ground.

Virgil began to pick it up as she cried, "Look for yourself! Are you happy now?" Her eyes were starting to pour out tears.

Virgil examined it and looked confused. "What am I suppose to see?"

"Look at the number on the top." She whimpered.

On the very top of the sheet was the number 90,000 was circled in bright red ink.

"I see a really big number…" Virgil stated flatly.

"You idiot! That's how many I sold in the first week!" Valerie started to bawl. Tears started to flow and she gasped for air like a little girl. "I only *sob*…sold *sob*…9...90…90,000…*sob*…"

Raquel was shocked at the girl's behavior. *Only 90,000 in a week? Poor you…*

"See this is how I get repaid. I used to think my readers were so loyal. Only 90,000 in a week. ONLY 90,000?!" She paused at started to cry even harder. "Do you know what this means Virgil?"

"Schuler…" He muttered under his breath.

"Yes," she bawled. "He'll kick me out of the department, just you watch!"

Raquel was quite drawn into this strange girl. She must have been an excellent writer yet she felt so insecure from a slight drop in book sales. It had nearly ruined her.

"I can see him now," Valerie continued the soliloquy, "he'll walk in here and say 'Sorry Ms. Dictorian, but I must ask you to no longer be part of this department. You will be asked to report to the Burn Out department where you shall await further instructions...' and he'll laugh and be off." She suddenly lurched out of her chair and screamed, "I don't want to go there Virgil! We both know that's where any writer on their last leg goes! I've got plenty of energy in me still. I can do it..."

"Okay Valerie, I'm sure he won't go that far..."

"You don't know that!" She grabbed the bottle of the desk and started to slowly drain the contents in greedy gulps. Valerie just as quickly put it down. "He'll be coming for me, he'll be coming..." She curled up in the fetal position on her chair cradling the bottle to her breast.

Virgil grabbed Raquel's hand. "I think it's best if we leave."

Raquel nodded, "I agree."

Valerie still sat on her chair saying the same haunting words: "He'll be coming for me…" until Virgil hastily shut the door. "I'm sorry you had to see that."

"It's okay but, I think she really needs help." Raquel looked back at the door. "Is everyone in this department like her?"

"Somewhat." Virgil looked kind of sad though. "They are mostly workaholics, but excellent writers. And one small slip up like that, they don't know how to handle it properly. The poor guys; Schuler's got them so wrapped around his finger that they act and behave as if there's nothing else to life but their work." He stopped walking halfway down the hall. Virgil studied the various names on the doors. "They end up wasting most of their lives writing. They 'write' their lives away, I guess you could say. One day they'll go to the bathroom and while washing their hands, look up in the mirror and see white hair, wrinkles, and the less fortunate ones, less hair, and they'll think: 'Where the hell'd all the time go? What was I doing with my life?' You see," They had approached an elevator at the end of the hall and Virgil pushed the little ↓ button. "Writing and all…it's great, it really is. It's lots of fun but when you allow it or anything else to get in the way of living, it's not worth it."

The elevator doors opened and Raquel and Virgil stepped in.

"But isn't your job a part of who you are? That means it was something to do with your life, right?" Raquel asked.

"Perhaps," Virgil said, "but you can't live life with your eyes facing downward all the time, now can you?"

*   *   *

Valerie had recognized Raquel in an instant. She slowly approached Christian and Raquel. Valerie gave Christian a brief hug and then turned to Raquel. "Miss Polanski, I must say that I apologize for behaving the way that I did the other day. It was very, err… inappropriate."

"No need to apologize Valerie; it was easy to see why you were so distressed the other day. I get it…"

"No, I'm afraid that I really do have to say I'm sorry Miss Polanski. Work is no excuse for a person to treat others like shit. I was behaving like I could control something that I ultimately had no control over."

Christian looked sadly at Valerie, "I heard you have departed from our presence at Ironwood Press."

"I'm afraid so Christian, but I'm actually enjoying it. Unemployment I mean; especially from that place. It's like a breath of fresh air."

"Really?" Christian only looked at her curiously.

"Yeah, I mean, I have no department I belong to, no rules to follow, no particular ways I have to write, no deadlines, just being lazy-old me."

"But how are you going to spend your life now? Miss Dictorian, you have written your entire life, I should feel as though you'd be so much more undone by your recent dismissal."

"Oh Christian," Valerie almost let out a little chuckle. "There's more to life than writing. I mean, I'm supposed to leave in a few days to take care of my mother, all the way out in Oregon, living all by herself. I really do think she'd really appreciate a little company. Besides, I have plenty of money set away to survive a while. It probably won't last the rest of my life, but hey, I'll probably write another time, only I will choose what I write, and won't let some group or even people's opinions control what it is."

Valerie smiled at Raquel and Christian. "I don't know why, but I feel so great now!" She started to skip away in the snow before she turned around. "Oh and I almost forgot, Happy New Year to you both!"

The couple smiled back and Raquel couldn't imagine for the life of her what had gotten into Valerie's head. At least she wasn't trying to live life with her eyes pointed down. Christian had suddenly grasped her wrist and whispered, "I think we need to get out of here."

"What…"

"There's a 1987 Back SS El Camino with dark tinted windows just over yonder. Do you see it?"

Sure enough Raquel saw it, parked on the very edge of the park; it seemed to be facing in their direction. Every hair on her body stood up.

"I noticed it this morning at the café, and later at your friend's bakery. I feel as though he's been observing our movements all day." Just as soon as Christian had finished, the car began to proceed forward and it began to move along, passing the park entirely. They quickly slipped off the bench and began to sink away into the fading afternoon light.

Sam Schiano sat in a 1987 Black SS El Camino while he watched Raquel Polanski and Christian

Martinez talk with some girl who seemed slightly delusional. *My luck, the target's involved with a big-shot writer and Ms. Schizo over there.* The delusional women soon ran away and the couple on the bench continued talking. Sam peered through his binoculars and watched the two up-close. Just as he began to watch, the Christian fellow seemed to turn his head and point Raquel straight into the binoculars. *Oh shit, they saw me.* Suddenly Sam found himself gunning the car into drive. He tried to inconspicuously escape his prey's glare. *The Christian fella knew all along. That little fucker...*

*　　　*　　　*

The Entertainment Department

Virgil and Raquel stayed in the elevator for the next two floors. Raquel couldn't help but noticed that the button right underneath the button for floor number nine was labeled **7+8** which made absolutely no sense.

Virgil offered an explanation. "The next two departments are given two floors worth of space. These guys are also bigwigs that earn a bunch for Schuler as well." The elevator started to whir down. "Unlike the C.O.T.C. department, you'll actually see people interacting and well, they may seem a bit rude. They tend to resent newcomers so just be polite and let me do the talking."

Raquel only nodded in agreement and waited as the elevator door began to open. She was amazed at what she saw. Instead of just one long hallway on the previous floor, the Entertainment Department was one large room. There were multiple T.V. monitors that completely covered one whole wall and each was set to a different channel with a dissimilar sporting event on each one. People buzzed around in flurry of activity. Young faces of both men and women anxiously watched the massive screens, holding nothing but a clipboard with paper in one hand and a pencil poised in another, furiously taking notes. The wall opposite the T.V. screens was a continuous row of desks and computers occupied by many of the young members. The same wall was made up entirely of a glass panel that allowed for a panoramic view of the New Yorkian December's snowfall.

Raquel noticed that everyone dressed the same. Men wore a smart black suit and the women wore a white blouse and a black skirt beneath it. They all looked exactly the same. The only difference that Raquel could distinguish between each face was various facial features and natural hair color. The men all wore the same crew-cut hairstyle but the women were allowed the privilege of being able to choose their own which resulted in hairstyles that were all very professional-looking. Even physique was hard to distinguish. Raquel immediately noticed that all the men were well-built. With the same broad shoulders and barrel chests that made them look like eye candy movie stars. They were not massive but healthily muscular. The women were the same way. They all had that perfect "Volleyball Body" as Raquel had heard of it; the kind of body every women dreamed of having. Strong legs, wide hips, a flat stomach, and a tan that was almost impossible to achieve in nature. *They're perfect.* Raquel could hardly take in the amount of human beauty.

Virgil had just started to speak. "Now this is one of the busiest departments. They are constantly watching every known sports channel from the U.S. and abroad trying to get as much info as they can. They specialize in written works regarding sports; like those fancy health magazines you always see at the grocery store."

Raquel was still taking in all the noise and the constant flurry of activity. People ran around in circles often multitasking. One of the funniest things she noticed was that everyone in the department addressed each other by their last names in conversation. She could occasionally catch snippets of commands and greeting being tossed around.

"Johnson, I need a copy of the report pronto…"

"Wallace, please go inform Jassol about the game…"

"Yo Remington, you see that game last night?"

"Smith, go let off some steam in the sauna."

"The sauna?" Raquel found herself wondering aloud.

"Oh yeah," Virgil started, "the Entertainment Department has its own mini-gym, a protein shake bar, locker room for members, and a sauna." He motioned towards a small area in the corner of the massive room where Raquel could make out a small glass-windowed room with the label: *Gym*, written above. Inside the gym, a young Adonis and Aphrodite ran side-by-side on a pair of treadmills and chatted while viewing a T.V. that had been placed in there for their enjoyment. Right next to the small room was two entrances that read: **Locker Rooms** and for each entrance was the universal symbol of either a cartoon man or woman.

Next to the locker rooms was the small smoothie bar Virgil talked about where several of the writers stopped to buy a smoothie from a young, unenthusiastic youth who worked the bar. On most days, more often than not, it was probably an intern.

While there was no one hallway dedicated to offices there were a few that resided above the smoothie bar and gym and were reachable by one small staircase situated right next to smoothie bar. One each window again the words: **Ironwood Press** much like the other offices in the C.O.T.C Department only this time it seemed like every office occupant was some type of editor. One door caught Raquel's attention which said *Chief Editor*. She was unable to make out the name before the door was flung open and someone came storming out.

"WHO THE HELL SCREWED UP THIS MONTHS EDITION!"

The reincarnation of Goliath the Philistine was standing upon the ledge. The raging individual had come out screaming the words in a bloodcurdling yell. He was a huge bulk of a man; taller than everyone else in the room and much more built up, with huge arms and thick legs that strained with every movement and a thick bulging neck where the veins seemed as though they would pop at any given minute. There was certain animal ferocity that burned in his eyes and his face had also taken a lovely medium-rare steak pink.

He bellowed out the same words again, "I SAID, 'WHICH ONE OF YOU IDIOTS SCREWED UP **MY** MAGAZINE?!" This time the words caused the whole room to freeze and every single head turned in his direction. He started to pace down the stairs and walk on ground level again. Several people started to cautiously approach him and offer consolation but he would push them aside.

Raquel shyly leaned over to Virgil and whispered, "Who's that?"

"That's the Chief Editor, kinda like the head guy here. Name's Hugh Jassol. Not the guy you want to cross paths with."

The giant Jassol had finally approached a nervous looking writer and yelled in his face, "ENTRICAN! Who wrote the section about dangerous workout equipment in this month's edition? Hmm Entrican? Who the hell did it? Can you tell me?"

Entrican only squeaked a quiet, "Vanders sir. He wrote it." To add measure to the effect he pointed to a young man that had been, at that moment, ordering something at the smoothie bar. Every head in the room turned to face him. Sweat started to drench Vanders' face in seconds.

Jassol turned to face him. "So it was you Vanders? Eh? Do you know what we do with people like you?"

The man answered, "N...no sir."

"You disgust me," Jassol sneered. He pointed to several other writers near Vanders. "Get his sorry ass outta here." He motioned towards the elevator doors that Raquel and Virgil had just exited sometime before.

"YES SIR!" the men answered in unison. In a flash the ordered men had each taken one of Vanders' limbs in hand and started to drag the sobbing, protesting man to the elevator.

Everything was silent in the room except for the cries of, "Please boss, I'll do it right next time! I really didn't mean to! It slipped my mind!" The men had finally arrived at the elevator and pressed the ↓ button. The doors opened and soon Vanders found himself flung inside despite his protests. The doors closed and the cries of the young man went silent.

Jassol looked around and shouted, "**WE** do not make mistakes! **I** do not tolerate mistakes! There will be no mistakes!"

With a religious reverence of a tent revival each man and woman was up on his/her feet and answered, "YES SIR!" In perfect unison.

Hugh Jassol only nodded. He then yelled, "Now back to work! They don't pay you to sit on your assess all day!"

Everyone resumed whatever they were doing before the little episode. Raquel just stood were she was, completely shocked at the chief editor's behavior. It was all so strange here.

Hugh Jassol had started to calm down. He suddenly caught Virgil and Raquel waiting in the crowd, standing out like a pair of sore thumbs. "Well Everley, who've you brought this time?"

"Her name is Raquel Polanski. She's currently looking to possibly publish here at Ironwood Press."

Instead of being formally introduced or shaking hands Jassol just stood there scrutinizing Raquel with his eyes. "You a pretty good writer Polanski?"

"Um, Mr. Schuler seemed to think so…"

"Oh you think you're that good?! Just you wait till you get in here. You'll find that everything you've written is children's stuff compared to what these boys and girls produce!" He swept his hand over the expanse of the room to indicate all the young and fresh minds.

"Oh sir," started Raquel, "I didn't mean to be arrogant. I was just telling you about Mr. Schuler's opinion about my writing."

"Sure." Jassol was in her face now. He was a very intimidating individual. Suddenly as if a change of character he reached out his hand with a smile and said, "Pleasure to meet you Polanski. Name's Hugh, Hugh Jassol, chief editor of this fine Entertainment Department and author of the best seller: *The Condensed History of Sports*."

Well here's my welcome, Raquel thought to herself but she only smiled and went along with it. She attempted to make some small talk with the chief editor. "Excuse me sir, but what does your department specialize in?"

"Sports magazines and the like. We make sure that the world outside stays up-to-date with all the latest news in sports. It is truly a fine department." He smiled as he watched the writers toil away with their note-taking and exercising.

Raquel still wanted to know about the uniforms and haircuts. "And sir one more question, why does everyone dress the same?"

"Oh that," Jassol smiled to himself. "It establishes the two single greatest feelings in this world: pride and unity. Yep, good ole' pride and unity are the best things one can feel Polanski. Let no one convince you otherwise." He again looked out over all the people in the room. "You see Polanski, I have a department that is only for *strong* boys and girls. If you keep 'em all in line they'll work together better. The 'uniform' look of the Entertainment Department is really masculine for the men, and very professional for the women." He paused and then sighed. "But you've gotta discipline 'em early so that they don't fall for that bullshit individualistic stuff preachers and New Age hippies try to teach the kids. It makes a man soft."

Raquel didn't think very highly of Jassol or his department and she certainly wasn't going to join it anytime soon.

"She must be a fine girl, isn't she?" Jassol was now facing Virgil who hadn't said but a word during the whole conversation.

"Yes Mr. Jassol, she's fine." His face started to blush a little.

"Well that's great! So Polanski, what do you write?"

"Well I've written this book, *The First Son* about a greedy prince and…"

"Stop right there." Jassol put a hand up to silence her. "You write *fiction*?! Ohh what a joke! I actually thought you wrote something serious like journalism or…" But his voice dissolved into a series of laughs accompanied by tears.

*Why I oughtta…*Raquel was suddenly interrupted by Virgil who motioned for her to follow him.

"I think it's time to go."

"I agree." She said exasperated.

"Oh fiction, not just any fiction, but fiction about old, dead historical figures. Oh I'd pay to see *that*!" Jassol was laughing so hard he had to steady himself on the shoulder or someone who was standing nearby.

His insults felt like little barbs being shot into Raquel and she hated it. Virgil tried to console her. "Don't listen to him. He's a big jerk to

113

everyone. Forget about it." He ushered her to small door that was on the complete opposite end of the room from the elevator. The door read: Social Department.

Virgil was trying to let Raquel in as fast he could while trying to console her. "Forget about it. It doesn't matter what he thinks. I'm sure your writing is just great." The door was finally opened and Raquel and Virgil stepped through. But even as Virgil was closing the door, she could still hear the thunderous, roaring laughter of Hugh Jassol.

*   *   *

They had almost run back to Christian's apartment. Upon entering the apartment they discovered that not everyone had left after the New Year's Party. A young man no higher than Raquel's chest was sipping lemonade at a dining room table. He smiled sheepishly at Raquel and cried out, "Oh I knew it Christian, you dirty man, you. Caught bringing home a woman; I see how it is…"

"Mr. Wagner, how dare you address Miss Polanski in such a manner. And I am not a whore-monger sir, need I remind you."

"Oh in that case, cheers Miss Panski!" He raised the bottle to his lips and took another swig.

"You've gotten into the hard lemonade again haven't you?" Christian was still standing in the doorway, looking more than unhappy.

The young only hiccupped and let out a childish laugh. "What lemonade?" He pretended to look thoroughly around the room. "I don't see any hard lemonade."

"I demand you give me that bottle or compensate me for the amount you have drunken."

"No."

"Mr. Wagner!"

Christian stamped off across the room and with his palm facing up and open. "Hand me the bottle immediately!"

"No!"

Suddenly Christian was reaching across the table to grab the bottle, only Mr. Wagner held the bottle behind him even further. Christian kept reaching before Mr. W's grasp slipped and the bottle smashed onto the floor.

"You've done it now, you bastard…" Christian turned around to look at Raquel, "I come in here and he's perfectly intoxicated." He quickly went to look for a dust pan while the drunk started to sprawl across the table to take a nap. Christian finally found something to clean up the mess in a cabinet. "Miss Polanski I regret I could not properly introduce you to my friend here. He is another agent in the Miscellaneous

116

Department. I present to you the ever inebriated Sean Wagner."

Mr. Wagner let out a small belch before he peered over at Raquel. "An' how you doin' Miss Panski?" He chuckled a little and fell back on the table.

Raquel didn't say anything but only watched as Christian proceeded to clean up the mess. He finished quickly and threw what remained of the bottle in the trash can. He then began to frantically look around for something.

"You need help?" Raquel finally stepped inside.

"Yes, yes, I need help finding my cellular device. I believe it was lost during last night's festivities. Oh where could it be?"

They searched the whole apartment more thoroughly than a jealous woman searching through her husband's phone history. All efforts prove futile. Raquel and Christian finally rendezvoused back at the kitchen and watched as Mr. Wagner still slept safe and sound. Christian hopped up and then walked over to the sleeping young man. "He probably has it. Yes indeed, he stole it from me at the last company yacht party and began to send obscene texts to the people I held dearest to my heart. Why he almost gave my poor aunt Alexis in Virginia a heart attack. She later said she believed I had joined a street gang and had decided to impress all my relatives with rather 'colorful language'." Christian turned to look at the boy. He delivered a soft poke in the ribs. "Mr. Wagner, oh Mr. Wagner. It's three o'clock in the afternoon, I think it's time you awaken and turn over my phone."

The sleeping boy only looked up quickly and groaned softly, "I don't have it, he does."

"Mr. Wagner, please elaborate on who *he* is…"

"Oh, you know, the guy with the dark glasses, the one who said he was part of the Feds and that he wanted to see your phone…"

"What do you mean *the guy with dark glasses*? Sean, I need more of an explanation!"

"The dude came in here for a little bit, poked around and then left."

"You mean you **let him in**?"

"No, the door was still open after Emily Stamboli left at around ten. The guy just walked into the doorway, saw me and said 'Mind if I come in?' So I said, 'Sure why not?' and so he did. That's about the same time he asked for your phone and I told him I had seen it on the counter earlier. He probably grabbed it and continued to look around the apartment. 'Course by then the room was already spinnin'."

Christian's eyes looked wide with fear. "Miss Polanski, I need to call my friend a cab and then we are going to leave here. Do you have everything you need in the case it becomes necessary we have to hide?"

Raquel could hardly speak; her day just kept getting weirder and weirder. She just nodded.

"Then let us proceed. I fear time may be running   out."

*   *   *

The Social Department

Raquel was so busy thinking about her encounter with Hugh Jassol that she hadn't even

119

noticed the surrounding room she and Virgil had stepped into.

"Presenting, the Social Department!" Virgil announced in a fanfare-like voice while his hand swept the expanse of the room. Just like the Entertainment Department the room was two stories tall but the décor was vastly different. The entire room was coated in a tacky coat of hot pink paint. Everything else in the room was colored pink: pink chairs, pink television monitors, pink pillows that lay strewn everywhere, and everyone (which meant *only* girls) wore the same outfit: low-cut pink t-shirts with matching pink short shorts (most of which had some girly symbol like a heart or smiley face, bedazzled on the buttocks pocket). Every girl wore pink sunglasses, pink lipstick, pink flip flops, and each and every nail had been painted with the same ghastly, neon, pink polish. The only individuality to be found among the girls was in their various hairstyles.

The layout was drastically different from that of the Entertainment Department. The Social Department had an outward-looking wall of windows that also allotted the same amount of space dedicated to panoramic views however, the visibility of those views had been completely obstructed. Every square inch of the windows had been plastered with posters of male celebrity heartthrobs posing for their adoring, female fans. Raquel noticed that various posters of the same nature had also been hung up on the walls around the room.

Like the Entertainment Department, there was one wall used specifically for television monitors, but these monitors displayed everything from social networking sights to camera shots of what Raquel guessed was the interior of the *Hawke* building. All the girls had flocked to one of the ground-level monitors and were starring at it intently.

"What are they doing?" Raquel whispered to Virgil not wanting to attract the attention of the girls.

"Well, you see, Schuler thought it'd be great if the company had a department that provided security for the company. However he wanted to call it something less intimidating than 'the Security Department' so he created the euphemistic: Social Department. The only purpose it serves is to monitor any 'suspicious activity' around the offices. I mean, who else to have snoop around the offices looking for anything abnormal other than a bunch of girls."

Raquel looked at the crowd of girls huddled around one of the monitors. She could hear occasional outbursts of shrieks and giggles emitting from the pink mob. "You mean, they actually take people down and all that?"

"Well not exactly." Virgil only smiled. "They just have to push some buttons, literally. All they do is sit around all day and watch for 'suspicious activity' and report immediately to the true security team downstairs, consisting of a few retired cops and the like and they're the ones who do the dirty work. These girls just act as a sort of eyes and ears in the company; especially for Schuler. They monitor everything from social media websites to the many screens you see before you, to get a glimpse into the life and habits of every author employed under Ironwood Press. If they see anything that Schuler labels as 'suspicious activity' they immediately report back to him."

"What do they define as 'suspicious activity'?"

"Who knows? That's on Schuler's terms." He glanced over at the bunch that was anxiously waiting for something to appear on one of the screens. "The only thing is, sometimes they abuse their power and use it for more personal reasons."

Raquel could hear various voices talking in hushed tones.

Towards the very front of the crowd, Raquel could just barely see a young girl seated directly in front of the ground level monitor. "I know he's doing it." She sneered, "I know he's going behind my back with someone else." The only thing visible on the monitor was a view of a hallway with a young man standing by himself, his arms crossed. He would anxiously glance up and down the hall occasionally, as if he was waiting for someone.

"Don't be a silly goose Brittany. I'm sure Jimmy would *never* go for someone other than *you*." It had been one of the girls standing towards the front of the crowd. Her comment was followed by an array of others:

"I bet you five bucks it's that girl from the mailroom…"

"Ohmigod, I know. She's *soooo* sluty. Did you *see* her outfit yesterday…"

"I think Jimmy's sweet; he'd *never* cheat on *you*…"

"What if it's another guy…"

"Ohmigod. Every one ssshhh!" Brittany commanded. As if she was going to hear something through the camera.

Raquel watched in stunned silence as the drama on the monitor unfolded. Suddenly, Jimmy wasn't the only one in the hall. A young girl had suddenly approached him and started to place his hands in hers. Within moments of touching one another, Jimmy suddenly had her pushed up against the wall, kissing her violently. The illicit lovers' hands showed no sign of self restraint.

"OH MY GOD! NO WAY IN HELL!!!" Brittany suddenly smashed her fist down on a red button that stood before the monitors. A small mike lay next to it. "SECURITY!!!" She screeched into it, "WE HAVE A CASE OF PDA ON THE FIRST FLOOR! I REPEAT, LEVEL C PDA!!!"

Within moments, the impassioned lovers had been separated by two security guards that had also appeared in the hall.

Brittany collapsed into an emotional wreck on her plush swivel chair. "He didn't love me!!!" She sobbed while tears streamed for her eyes causing black rivers of mascara to flow down her cheeks.

Several of the girls padded her on the back offering consolations like:

"Don't worry; he was *totally* not on your level…"

"It's okay, Jimmy's a man-whore anyways…"

"Just be glad it wasn't another guy…"

Others were wondering what happened:

"Oh…my…god…who was it?"

"I didn't get to see it…"

"Who, Brittany? Tellmetellmetellme WHO!?"

Raquel was disgusted by their actions.

"Jessica Harris is a skank!" Brittany bawled out and she burst into even more tears.

"It's all right girls. We know what we have to do now." One of the older girls had begun to address the entire room. "One of our sisters has betrayed one of her very own with the ultimate sin of... skankiness!"

Several gasps could be heard and one girl exclaimed an "Oh no!"

"Oh yes!" The girl continued, "And we all know the punishment for that, don't we?" The speaker continued.

"Eternal shunishment!" One young enthusiastic girl yelled.

"Very good Larissa." The speaker said, "From hence forth, not one of you shall associate with, talk to, make eye contact, eat with, text, call, email, right letters to, send Christmas cards to, go to the movies with, hangout with, go shopping with, get a makeover with, party with, cry with, laugh with, or show any such emotion with, dream with, or even think about the sister we once knew as Jessica Miller Harris." With that, the zealous girl walked over to a large chalkboard in the middle of the room that Raquel hadn't noticed before. On it was written in girlish cursive, was every single girls' name in the Social Department. The speaker (who Raquel now took to be the head of the department) snatched up a piece of chalk. "For henceforth, let it be known that Jessica Miller Harris is subject to…" She paused for dramatic effect. "ETERNAL SHUNISHMENT!" She raised the piece of chalk and put a slash through the name 'Jessica M. Harris'.

For a moment everyone in the room was silent. Then the speaker turned and faced everyone with a bright smile. "Now sisters, let us forget this awful tragedy and return to our everyday routine." She walked over to Brittany who was still in tears on her chair and offered a warm pat on the back. "Now dear, how about you go to the bathroom and clean up a bit?" Unbeknownst to Brittany, her tears and mascara had painted war stripes on her face. She got off the chair and walked away.

The girls slowly trickled away from the scene, giggling and whispering as they plopped down in several bean bags (pink of course).

Raquel noticed that where the Social Department lacked in chairs it made up in bean bags that the girls would snuggle into while holding a smart phone in hand, a coffee in the other, snooping into people's private lives through the single greatest invention of social media.

No one had even bothered to pay any attention to Virgil and Raquel who had remained silent the whole time. The speaker suddenly turned around and noticed the two guests. "Oh, we have visitors!" She smiled, "I'm sorry you had to see that. Just a little girl drama, that's all." Her facial expression suddenly changed to one of utter disappointment. "Oh if it isn't Icky Virgil the Intern. And who's Ms. Plain Jane you brought along?"

Virgil started to defend himself and Raquel, "She has a name Victoria. This is Raquel Polanski, she's an upcoming author. Raquel, this is the Social Department head, Victoria Kilder."

Raquel made a slight nod in Victoria's direction.

"Are you trying to get her in our group, Virgil? 'Cause it's *sooo* not going to happen."

Victoria sopped to examine some of her fingernails. "There are requirements to be in the Social Department. First off, you have to think like all of us. Second off, you have to do everything like us. Outfits have to be the same, and you can only buy certain brands. Last off, you have to be pretty."

The last statement was a blow to Raquel, worse than the one from Hugh Jassol. Virgil was starting to refute her. "I'll have you know she's better than this little department of your's Victoria. Maybe you people would have more members if you weren't such a bitch!"

Victoria only sneered. "Haha, go away Icky Virgil the Intern. And take Little Ms. Nothing with you." She turned her nose. Several of the girls who had been watching started to giggle.

Raquel could feel the anger mounting inside of her. Maybe she had to worry about Hugh Jassol's size but Victoria was damn well near her own…

Virgil suddenly blurted out, "I've been dating one of you department members!"

It seemed as if the whole world had stopped spinning. Victoria's eyes grew enormous. "What...did...you...just...say?"

"I said," Virgil began, "I'm dating one of your department members."

"Who the hell..." Victoria began.

Virgil had motioned to a girl who was seated on a bean bag. It was the same girl who had answered Victoria's question so eagerly, the one named Larissa.

Victoria was in shock. "Larissa, is this true!?"

"Yes," Virgil snapped. He was now holding hands with Larissa. "And there's nothing you can do that will make that go away."

Victoria was smoldering but she decided to play it cool. She smiled wryly. "Larissa dear, what did I say about girls who date ugly boys? They're just sluts who throw themselves at any man who comes their way so they can be used."

"That's not true." Virgil yelled out. "I love her and she loves me."

Victoria continued to push. "Please Larissa, stop this nonsense and just say you don't love him."

"Baby, you know this is nuts. We've loved each other for such a long time." Larissa found herself caught in the tug-of-war between two voices.

"Larissa you must do as I say…"

"Come on honey, she doesn't know what she's talking about."

"You know what he's really after…"

"I *love you*."

"I will subject you to eternal shunishment."

Suddenly Larissa slowly started to drift away from Virgil.

"Where you going?" He asked.

Larissa bowed her head. "I…I…" She couldn't get the words out.

"That's it sweetie, take your time just let the words flow out: 'I don't love Virgil Everley.'" Victoria coaxed.

"I…I…don't love Virgil Everley." Larissa muttered.

"What? Larissa you don't mean…" Virgil was starring at her; Raquel noticed that his eyes had started to water.

"I said I don't love you, goddamn it!" Larissa had run off crying.

Victoria only smiled. Virgil was too heartbroken to even be angry. He only starred off in the direction Larissa had run off to.

"You heard her," Victoria said. "She doesn't love you. Now shoo fly shoo." She flicked her hand.

Raquel was in shock. She had just seen a heart broken in a matter of minutes. She couldn't get the image out of her mind: the look on Larissa's face as she told Virgil she didn't love him anymore. The poor girl was trying to survive; to remain on the same social status. It required that she sacrifice quite a bit: her emotions, her opinions and even some of her relationships. Possibly even her dreams. The only problem was that it had required her love, something of so high value, because of what her friends thought, for all too little the price. But after all, who wouldn't fear eternal shunishment?

*   *   *

Raquel stared out of her hotel window. The city buildings glistened in the last rays of light, as the first sun of the New Year began to set and darkness began to across the city. *New York looks so pretty in the right light*. There was a slight knock on the door and Raquel jumped. After Sean had told Christian about the unwanted guest in the apartment the two had immediately left. Christian evicted Sean, took a small suitcase of clothes and money, and proceeded with Raquel to the *Harrison Hotel* not but a few blocks away. They checked out two rooms and decided to contact the authorities as soon as possible. However the authorities who did manage to talk to Raquel and Christian could not help in anyway. So Christian and Raquel were all alone.

Christian had just stepped out for groceries and promised to return within the hour. "Don't fret Miss Polanski. It's only me, Christian." Raquel quickly went up to the door and checked through the peephole just for good measure. She undid the latch and let Christian in. He carried two grocery bags and a small book was tucked underneath his arm. Christian quickly set down

134

the groceries on a table near the door and proceeded to sit down.

"Hey Christian?"

"Yes Miss Polanski?"

"I need to talk to you right now."

"Yes, what about?"

Raquel sat herself down on the bed opposite the chair and began to speak, "I know we're in this really dangerous situation right now and I really appreciate how you're trying to keep us safe and all but I still need to do one more thing. I *need* to find the *other* Christian."

Christian only hung his head. "Miss Polanski, we cannot entertain the idea of that email being authentic at the present. For all we know it could have been written by someone claiming to be your former lover."

"I know it's dangerous. But what if it's actually him? What if Christian is still out there and he ends up spending the entire night waiting for me, but I never get there? I've hurt him before and I went through my life wondering if I could possibly set things right. You see, I've screwed up a lot of stuff and I just have to talk to him."

"Miss Polanski, I cannot allow you to do this. It's too much of a risk…"

"Please Christian, I just really need to do this. Please, I'll thank you so much when this is over…"

Christian was simply shaking his head. "I understand how well intentioned you are but I cannot allow you to gamble with your life. Not over some boy you once loved a long time ago."

Raquel was starting to become upset. She could feel a sense of anger begin to well up in her. "Oh I see how it is. You're just jealous."

"You know that that is not true…"

"Christian Martinez is just jealous that he was never able to fall in love properly."

"I would appreciate it, if you did not address me in such a manner…"

"Or maybe it's because you never had a chance to make things right? Huh, Christian? Is that it?"

"Shut up…"

"Is it because now I have a chance at doing something you never could? Maybe because I didn't screw up my relationships…"

"I said SHUT UP!" Christian was suddenly on his feet. Sweat moistened his forehead and tears were welled up in his eyes. Veins stuck out of his neck and the room seemed to be filled with the very sound of his pulse. "Do not tell me that I know nothing of love! Because I know too damn well how much it hurts! You don't understand. Every time I care about something I end up losing it." He began to calm down just a little. His breath began to slow down and his eyes became soft again. "You would only understand that I only care enough for you to protect you, if you understood everything I've ever lost." Christian sat down again and placed his head in his hand.

*   *   *

The End of Everley/The Pacifier/Serena Centre

"Good Morning ladies and gentlemen of Ironwood Press. We would just like to make a quick notification that The Pacifier will be open

*for an 11:30-12:00 session with today's guest:
DJ IcedT. Everyone is invited and **strongly
encouraged** to come. Thank you and have a
wonderful day."*

The whole situation had been interrupted in a
single announcement.

"OH…MY…GOD! GIRLS, WE HAVE, TO
GO!" Victoria Kilder's face had suddenly lit up
as she shrieked.

Before Raquel could even recall her train of
thoughts that had been interrupted at that point,
she was suddenly facing an onrush of shrieking,
giggling and annoying girls rushing for the
Entertainment Department door. They didn't
even pay one ounce of attention to her or Virgil.
After a minutes worth of stampede, Raquel and
Virgil were left alone in the room.

She felt terrible for the poor intern. How was
she supposed to go on a tour with someone who
had just had their heart broken?

"I'm really sorry," she started. "If you want I
can just end the tour and tell Mr. Schuler that I
had to leave early or…"

Virgil put up his hand to silence her, "It's…okay. We can continue, it's just that…." Virgil struggled to find the right words, "We were really in love…or at least I thought so…and yet…she threw it all away. Just like that."

Raquel noticed that his head was bowed like those who have been defeated and are ashamed.

"Really we can stop and I'll be the one…"

"No, I can go on. It'll help distract me for awhile." He managed to look up with a weak smile.

"Okay. But only if you're really sure."

They exited by way of the Entertainment Department which now stood empty and void of any noise whatsoever. Raquel found it kind of creepy.

"So what's this *Pacifier* thing that everyone got so hyped up about?"

"*The Pacifier* is like one big dance room, complete with turning tables for a DJ, crappy pop music, tiles that change color, disco ball, strobe lights, tons of food, and plenty of drinks."

"So basically like a normal party?"

"Kinda. Schuler got the idea after some bad PR stuff started affecting the company because of several authors. DUI's, drug possession, people being found on rooftops, it got really bad at one point." They continued walking through the room. "So Schuler decided what if he got 'all the party outta their systems' or at least that's how he put it. Why don't we just let everyone party like there's no tomorrow for about half an hour each week and then they'll behave more? Sure enough it worked. Within a month of *The Pacifier* opening, people started to clean up their acts out in public and did all their dirty work safely within the confines of the company. They don't have to worry about cops and from the few times I went, there's all the sneakiness of every party you went to in high school. Liked spiked Hawaiian punch and what not."

It puzzled her, why people had even wanted to even to attend such parties? "Why do you think people have to do stuff like that?"

Before Virgil could answer he was cut off by a deep, baritone voice that pierced the air, "Yo Everley! Ya got something we need?"

Raquel turned to face a set of 5 muscle toned guys who had just emerged from the locker rooms wearing nothing but towels tied around their waists. Regardless that Raquel found these guys attractive, something about them felt very ominous.

"He..he..hey guys. I'm sorry." Stuttered Virgil, "I didn't know you guys wanted money today." Virgil, who had just a few moments before had his heart broken was now trembling, every last inch of him.

"Ya idiot." It was the head man. "We made a deal. Ya pay us lunch money every Friday. Ya skipped out on us last time and don't tell me ya forgot about dis time too? Whatta stoopid a something?"

"Really Victor, I…I…can explain besides…."

"Eye, who da sweet treat wit 'im?" Victor motioned towards Raquel. "Ya got yerself a new babe Evereley?"

"No, I just…was leading…she's suppose to be a new writer." The words came out uneasily.

"Ya forgot? Didn't ya?" Victor turned red in the face, "Maybe little miss ova der can pay off ya debt four ya?" Victor and his gang started to approach the couple. "Ya betta 'ope she eider got a big wallet or up for whole lotta lovin' to pay ya debts, 'cause afta dis I'm gonna use ya sorry ass to wipe the flor!" Suddenly all the men were charging Raquel and Virgil.

"Run!" Virgil cried.

He grabbed her hand and they started sprinting for the elevator door that was only a few yards away. Suddenly Virgil came to a complete stop.

"Are you nuts?! They're right behind us!" Raquel pointed towards the group of oncoming men.

"Leave me. The elevator door won't open in time and I can stall them. You can make it."

"Are you insane? Because it doesn't sound like Mr. Mafia over there plans on giving you a hug."

"Please just run. I know what I'm doing." He smiled. "It's been a pleasure knowing you Raquel. I hope we do meet again." Raquel was still dumbfounded. "Now run!"

Raquel ran with all her might (or as much as she could in the high heels she chose for today); a small glimpse behind her revealed Virgil grabbing a nearby aluminum chair and heaving it full force at the first assailment who then promptly crumbled onto the floor along with the chair. Virgil was then pummeled by the second man with a blow to the face. The others gathered around the downed body of Virgil while Victor continued running. "You guys take care of 'im. I'll get da gurl."

Ten feet...six feet...four feet...almost there... Once she arrived at the doors Raquel began hitting the 'open' button with a ferocity that was bit overly frantic but as chance would have it the doors opened at that moment.

She stepped in and started to hit the 'close doors' symbol nearly jamming her thumb. *Come on you stupid machine, close already damnit!"*

"I'll make sure ya pay off Everley's debts…"

The doors started to close. *Yes please God, close the doors. There almost done.*

"...I'll make sure ya little boyfriend gets it good. What da 'ell are you doin' closin' dose doors..."

Yes...almost there. The door was a few inches from being shut and Victor was just a few inches away from arriving.

"Gotcha!" A giant meaty hand had been placed between the two doors. Within seconds Raquel used all her might to kick the hand connecting her heel into one of the fingers and pushing with all her might. There was a high pitched squeal and the doors shut.

She lay on her back now, starring up at the elevator ceiling. A light sweat drenched her forehead and she was breathing rapidly. Raquel started to worry over Virgil and what had become of him. She was also clueless as to where she should head next. As she pondered over all this the one thing that kept popping up was that ugly hand inserting itself between the elevator doors. Never before had she been gladder to have worn heels.

Lights flashed in a non-epileptic friendly matter, an auto tuned pop sung screeched out of the giant stereo speakers with lyrics along the lines of 'we should dance because it could very well be our last day on earth'. There were three giant tables that were piled with bowls that had been packed to the gills with snack-sized food, and two more separate tables devoted solely to several Gatorade buckets, that one often seen at sporting events, filled with concoctions of Kool-Aid mix and God-only-knows amounts of Vodka. People were jumping up and down along with the beat of the music, sweat dripping off their bodies. Not a single blip of oxygen existed between the dancers as they moved about in any lewd position possible.

The DJ of the week was overseeing the festivities while yelling into a small mike the few party mantras like: "If you're having fun right now throw your hands in the air!" To which people would respond with all sorts of 'whoops' and 'yeah's and an array of all sorts of yells and shrieks that bordered on almost primitive.

In the corner, leaning against the wall all by herself was Serena Centre. She had her arms crossed in a cold-mannered way while holding a cup of Kool-Aid that was too spiked to enjoy. It tasted awful. *Look at all this shit*, she thought to herself. *The company spends thousands of dollars on what: a giant orgy that's what. This is such shit*. Serena couldn't help being cynical, it was part of her nature.

Born and raised as a Mid-Western small-town girl, Serena hailed from some place in Nebraska. Right out of high school Serena had no intentions of staying in what she called "the most boring city on earth" so she "blew outta that popsicle stand" and ended up in the Big Apple as an attempted writer. She had wanted to publish some memoir she had written about small-town life that had been submitted to Ironwood Press only to come back a few days later with a lovely little rejection letter that came back:

DEAR MS. CENTRE,

I'M AFRAID THAT I CANNOT POSSIBLY MAKE AN ATTEMPT TO PUBLISH YOUR WORK AT THIS TIME. IT IS OF POOR QUALITY, LACKS PATHOS, AND IS EXTREMELY DULL. IN A MORE TRUTHFUL SENSE, IT JUST SUCKS. THANK YOU FOR YOUR ATTEMPT AT WRITING.

SINCERELY,

COLIN WILLIAMS

(LITERARY AGENT-MISCELLANEOUS DEPARTMENT)

Needless to say the letter enraged Serena so much she went down to the *Hawke* building and made her way up to Schuler's office where she proceeded on a seven minute soliloquy about how "hurt" she was by the letter and that she could not believe that he would allow anyone from Ironwood Press to send such a "deplorable, gruesome, nasty, emotionally-scarring" letter to an upcoming writer. Most staff and security had been shocked by the girl's brute way of pushing through anyone and anything to get what she wanted but after the red-faced Serena had stopped ranting Schuler just laughed and said, "I like this girl's spunk. You're hired!" And that was how Serena Centre started working for Ironwood Press...as an intern.

At first she had been allured by the "You're hired" statement but apparently that also went so far as to include internship. *Okay my writing sucks.* She thought. *But c'mon, an INTRERN?! Just an **Intern**?! I ought to sue somebody. Oh and if I ever meet that Mr. Williams, the plans I have for that man*...Serena Centre stood alone thinking creepily sadistic thoughts to herself until she was approached by a slightly drunk, fairly tall, young man from the Entertainment Department.

"Ey babe, wanna dance?"

Serena only made an obscene hand gesture at him. The young man, discouraged, stumbled off elsewhere in a sad attempt to hit on another girl.

The guys here are such creeps and not even that good looking. Serena scanned the dance floor. *If I want to climb up the social status ladder here I got to do something great.* The music pulsed on. *Maybe if I actually, like, help someone maybe then they'll pay attention.* The terrible song started to change into another song with the same tempo and an awful assortment of lyrics. At that moment Serena noticed that the pair of elevator doors on the other side of the room opened and a girl walked into the room looking rather confused and lost. *Oooo, who's she? She looks new. Isn't she suppose to have, like, a guide or something? Could I help her?* Then the revelation came. *Wait so if she's lost and I help her then maybe Walrus Schuler will be like, 'Thank you Ms. Centre your deeds have earned you a job as an editor!' And I'll act all, 'Oh Mr. Schuler I couldn't. I mean, I didn't do **that** much!' And he'll be like, "Oh but Ms. Centre you must! After all someone like yourself deserves so much praise."*

Serena's daydreams had directed her attention from the situation unfolding right in front of her. The lost girl (Raquel Polanski) was being hit on by the same drunk guy who had approached Serena earlier. He now had Raquel by the arms and was swinging her around incessantly. It took some time before Serena came back to reality. *Oh no, that perv's got to girl. Time for my heroic rescue.*

She approached the dancing couple listening to Raquel's voice yelling out above the music, "Really dude, I don't know how comfortable I am with this!"

Serena tapped the big guys back while avoiding any bodily contact with people dancing around her. He turned around, "Whaaa?"

"Hey bub, the girl said she didn't want anyone swinging her around, now screw off."

"It's okay," the drunk said, "look she's havin' toons of fuunn..." To which Serena could see Raquel shaking her head back and forth rather zealously.

"Let go of her!"

"Or what?" He teased.

"This." In a single instant Serena had connected her nails to the left side the drunk's face and he released his grip while clutching his face.

"OWWW!" The giant started moving around blindly while trampling over people. Some of the girls were starting to scream now and there was a fairly large amount of noise that started to drown out the pulsating base of the music. The giant had crashed into several of the Gatorade buckets sending them crashing to the floor with a fair amount of brightly colored alcoholic beverage rushing in waves on people's feet.

"MY SHOES!" One girl shrieked which Raquel recognized as the voice of Victoria Kilder screaming.

There was a mad dash towards the elevator. People pushed and shoved but most of them were slipping on the wet floor bringing others around them down as well, like some sort of grotesque domino effect. The giant was still lumbering around clutching the left side of his face until he promptly sat himself down on one of the tables devoted to snacks.

During the whole ordeal Serena had pushed Raquel safely against one of the walls as they watched everyone run around like chickens without heads.

"THAT LITTLE BITCH NEARLY SCRATCHED MY EYE OUT!" It was again the giant who now sat sobbing on the table.

"Ladies and Gentlemen. I really need you all to stay calm..." DJ IcedT was making an attempt to appease the crowd but his announcement was cut off by a loud *CRACK!*

Everyone turned to face the source of the sound. The very same table that Mr. Giant had sat on couldn't take the weight and had snapped at the base sending a bowl of Chex Mix catapulting through the air and straight at the unsuspecting DJ, who had little time to take cover and whose head collided with the bowl in a solid *THUNK!*

Raquel could help but feeling a little panicky at the entire chaos of it all. Not one person in the room was on their feet or acting naturally. The whole scene was madness. It seemed like a good long while before a set of house lights replaced the seizure-inducing ones and a strange woman had just walked into the room. She was wearing a smart looking, navy-blue suit and had a gorgeous set of blonde curls that fell to the sides of her head.

"You all ought to be ashamed of yourselves." The women viewed the room disdainfully. The whole dance floor had been turned into one massive collection of bodily limbs, heads stuck in armpits, legs sticking out and flailing around like fish, and hands covering other's faces. The floor was littered with an array of snacks and a mixture of drinks that turned into a very unhealthy color. The elevator couldn't even close because of the amounts of people stacked up in between the doors. Shoes were strewn about the place and several male party goers appeared to be shirtless.

"I want everyone to report back to his or her department." It was the mystery woman again. "I am disappointed in seeing that you have allowed for your humanly instincts to get out of control. Just imagine what kind of social damage could have been done if this had been done outside this building. I will be letting your department heads know how shameful your behavior has been."

Everyone started to untangle themselves and march their sweat- and/or drink- drenched bodies towards the elevator. People began to leave in small waves. Raquel couldn't help but noticed how sad everyone looked: like chastised children. As the room slowly started to empty and Raquel and Serena were the only ones left except for their drunk acquaintance who was just now getting off the floor after a fainting spell.

Mr. Giant looked around the room and noticed the girls. "It's not my fault Mrs. Penny; it was that annoying little intern Centre and her friend." He pointed an ominous finger towards the two girls and then motioned to two parallel gashes along his left cheek that reminded Raquel vaguely of something from Jurassic Park.

"Is this true?" Mrs. Penny was now facing the two girls.

Serena started to answer, "Yeah but the perv started to hit on us and what was I supposed to let him do?"

"Young woman, I will not tolerate language such as 'perv' thrown about in this establishment and as for you Mr. Sanders." She turned to the young man, "I will make sure Mr. Jassol deals with you and your blatant promiscuity."

"But I…"

"I don't want to hear excuses, young man. Now go to your department!"

Sanders waddled away to the elevator all the while giving Serena and Raquel dirty looks.

Once he was gone Mrs. Penny proceeded to address the girls, "Ms. Centre, I will need for you and your friend, excuse me if that offends you but I do not know your name." She was looking at Raquel who quickly answered, "It's Raquel, Raquel Polanski."

"Well I would like for you two young ladies to report to my office this instant. Please follow me." She motioned for them to follow. Serena huffed and started to walk over to follow Mrs. Penny but Raquel was a bit more hesitant to do so.

The Pacifier had taken an entirely new eerie tone. Raquel noticed that the DJ was still laying unconscious next to the turning tables and that the music continued to play. Something must have hit the machine for the stereos kept repeating a line of the song that reminded her of the whole situation.

"Yeah live it up

Now pour some in my cup

Live it up (Yeah)

Live it up (Yeah)"

        *   *   *

Christian had managed to speak again. "If you haven't noticed Raquel, I have a way of losing everything I love in this life; the things and people that I love are in fact the first to go. And poor Sonya, why poor Sonyna, who was so lovely, so immaculate drifted away from me. I understand that I am in fact the opposite of a magnet, I repel things."

"Love is in fact such a fluid thing that it is here one day, and gone the next! And yet strangely enough I find that for all its' uncertainty, love is still worth it. "

"Some people may claim I had a tragic life. That perhaps all the things I ended up destroying, were also the things I loved. I however, think I am triumphant, yes. Because is it not better to have love and to have lost than to never have loved at all?"

Christian now sat with tears in his eyes as he slowly looked at Raquel. "I may not have a lot of control in my life but what I would like do is protect those that I do...care for."

Raquel suddenly looked back up at him. "You've hardly known me for a few weeks; why do you feel so strongly about me?"

"Perhaps because you are different. But don't mistake me Miss Polanski, I shall never return to love in that sense. I know I am only bound to fail once again. You are one of my last good companions and I don't wish to lose someone again."

Raquel felt tears in her eyes. "I know Christian but I have to go. I need to fix something. I know you feel so strongly about taking care of people but you need to let me do this." Christian just sat back in his chair and didn't say anything after that. He slowly put his head his hands and stayed like that. Raquel did not stay to look, or to talk any longer. She quickly walked out of the room, through the hotel and onto the cold streets. All the while, salty tears were brimming in her eyes.

*   *   *

The Public Relations Department

Mrs. Penny led the girls through a small set of doors that had been placed on the wall opposite

158

the elevator which led into a long, narrow hall, much like the C.O.T.C Department only greatly different. The place was in complete disarray. Papers were scattered everywhere, people loomed about in the halls walking with no place to go, and the walls were covered to the very tee with various theatrical posters of musicals such as: *Wicked*, *The Phantom of the Opera*, *Miss Saigon, RENT*, and many more.

Raquel couldn't help but inquire as to the new department that lay before her.

"The Theatre Department," Serena answered looking as cheerfully as she could, "Mrs. Penny is kinda a part of it."

"Part of it?"

Mrs. Penny stepped over several scattered papers and pulled out a set of keys that let her into a room that read: **Jennifer Penny- Public Relations Department**. The door opened and she motioned with her hand for the girls to come in.

It was a strange office but highly organized compared to the chaotic hallway outside. Everything about it was highly organized. Everything from pencils and pens to documents and various manuscripts were filed away *in* cabinets *in* alphabetical order. Another oddity about the office was that it was a bit more spacious than the others and contained a giant mahogany wardrobe along with a mirror lined with light bulbs, the type that were found in actors' dressing rooms.

Mrs. Penny walked over to the mirror and sat herself down by the mirror.

"Please girls take a seat. This will only take a second." And as if she forgot something, "Oh Raquel please *do* shut the door."

Raquel secured the door and then took a seat by the desk along with Serena. She turned her head to watch in horror as Mrs. Penny performed a ritual that was almost like undressing.

A steady hand moved up and removed a blonde wig from her scalp which revealed an ugly, dull brownish, straight hair that had been matted down from the wig. Then she started to pull on the forehead and peeled off a flesh-colored mask from her face. Mrs. Penny had transformed from the beautiful businesswoman she was just a moment ago into a plain-Jane girl who was far from attractive. She wiped off the lipstick from her mouth with a small hankie then turned to face both the girls.

"Oh my god Serena; I tell you this job is sooo exhausting." Her voice had even changed to something with a twinge of deep southern drawl.

Raquel was thoroughly confused, "Um...did you just...I thought you were..."

"Oh honey, sorry to confuse you. My name's not really Jenny Penny." The women walked over to her desk and slipped off her stilettos and proceeded to sit while resting her feet on the top of the desk. "I'm not even married." She laughed and slipped off the ring from her left hand and placed in some drawer within the desk. "The name's Krystal Stephana. I work as part of the Public Relations department here, or should I say...I am the department head."

Raquel was still lost as ever. "Where's the Public Relations Department? You're the head? How? I thought that...wait...what?"

Stephana had reached into her pocket and had produced a pack of cigarettes that she started to fumble with. "You see dear, there is no set location for the lovely Public Relations Department. ***Everybody*** at Ironwood Press is part of the Public Relations Department. Yessiree, every author, editor, agent and the like has their own little piece of PR to do. It's all about how you present yourself." She was now lighting one of the cigarettes. "If you look your best, people will like you. That's why a better dressed guy is more likely to get the job than somebody who dressed poorly. It's why you wear the best black suit you can find to a relatives funeral and not your workout clothes. It's why most people fall in love with each other usually when they look their best. And that's why you most *definitely*, **never** wear your pajamas in public." Krystal let out one large *BURP!* and then continued with her soliloquy. Her crudeness appalled Raquel.

"You see, it's all about **respect**. I use to think one could show *respect* by loving one another. However, I figured that it's all in the looks and threads honey." She pointed to her business jacket and nodded, the small cigarette smoke wavering back and forth. "You know, it reminds me of that story they use to tell me in Sunday school. You've probably heard it; you know that Bible story where Adam and Eve, the first people, don't listen to God so they get kicked outta paradise? And do you remember one of the byproducts of their disobedience? They had to wear *clothes*. Yes, I believe God could not have been wiser in his punishment. Maybe Adam and Eve didn't foresee it, but God did. He thought, 'You want to disobey me? Then I shall punish you in one of the worst ways possible: I shall give you clothes, and fashion, and conformity, and teasing, and bullying, and ugly Christmas sweaters, corsets to squeeze the air out you, shoes to give you blisters and wet t-shirt contests. I shall give you lingerie, and adult boutiques, and every sort of clothing to please your imagination.'

Krystal leaned back further in her chair and jingled the cigarette in her teeth. Raquel thought that Stephana's thoughts were rather interesting. The whole fake mask and hair were still haunting her mind. "Excuse me, Mrs. Penn...I mean Ms. Stephana, but could you please explain why the wig, and the mask, and why are you in the Theatre Department?"

"Oh yes, I sure can honey." She smiled a little and then flicked the cigarette into small ashtray. "Schuler puts terrible pressure on all the writers here to maintain a perfect public image. Even if it means you become something you're not. Look at me. You're wondering why I'm located in the Theatre Department. Quite simply, I'm an actress and a very good one. When Schuler decided to come up with Public Relations he decided he needed someone to oversee it.   And who better that an excellent actress to show how good-hearted Ironwood Press really was. Of course as you can imagine I'm not very pretty." Raquel was about to open her mouth but Krystal beat her to it, "Oh please don't say, 'Don't beat yourself up.' or 'You're beautiful the way you are.' I know that I'm ugly. There's nothing worse in this world than an ugly person who thinks they're beautiful. I have already established in my head that by society's standards I'm far from being a piece of eye-candy."

"You see Raquel; most of how we get by in this life is based on what other people think of you. That's why it's one of the most important things to make sure that other people like you. It doesn't matter if you're not *yourself*. When someone dare display his raw, human emotions in front of someone, they hate him for it. Because," there was a brief pause in which

Krystal slid her feet down from the table and started to sit straight-up in the chair. "It reminds them of themselves. He suddenly notices the same common emotions that affect us all and how he's united to the atrocious man before him. Clothes, make-up, and everything like it serve to cover up emotional filth and portray to us as someone who is lovely. True, it serves as a more plastic version of that person but still more lovely."

There was something in Raquel that made her feel that all this stuff was wrong. "But Ms. Stephana with all due respect, I really thought it was the conditions of somebody's heart that counts."

A huge laugh elicited from Krystal. "Ha! Most people these days are only looking at surface value. Screw your sentimental and sappy 'it's what's on the inside that counts'! It is *so* much easier to love things that are lovely on the surface. It's very hard to *love* something that is deeply un*love*ly."

*   *   *

Raquel could feel something deep within her. It was the knowing sense of guilt that tugged at her heart with every step she took. She had abandoned Christian, her hope, and what may have been her last refuge. Surely the email had been sent by the *other* Christian and not by someone else out there, someone with the possible intention of hurting her. But such things are dismissed by those who are in love.

After all a wise man once said: "Love is a serious mental disease."

*   *   *

The Theatre Department//Serena Slips (literally)

The desk phone started ringing. Mrs. Penny (Krystal Stephana) answered with a, "Hello...I mean...hello." Her voice had faltered for a second as she had to switch from being a cynical Krystal Stephana into the perfect Mrs. Jennifer Penny. "Good afternoon sir...oh yes, I sent out a text about the *Pacifier* incident...yes everyone involved will be punished thoroughly...did I hear about what...no sir...why, that's terrible..." She started to feign fake genuine surprise and disgust, "I do hope they were punished...so the media is already here?!...yes, yes...I will be there right away...Have I seen a girl?...Her name wouldn't happen to be Raquel Polanski, would it?...oh yes she's hear safe and sound...let her make a statement to the media?...No that would be awful PR...I will do my best to cover it...yes I know, each of the young men involved will have their own statement...don't worry about it Mr. Schuler...I will do my best...bye."

Krystal set down the phone and then looked over at the girls, "Well damn it. I thought me and you would have a little chat for a while but I had to explain to this poor girl what Public Image is all about and now the media demands to see Mrs. Penny. Please allow me to offer my condolences as to what happened in the Entertainment Department earlier."

Raquel's eyes went wide, "Where's Virgil? Is he okay? How's he doing? What happened to those jerks?"

"Please one question at a time dear girl." Krystal held up her hand. "Yes Mr. Everley is in transit to the ER as we speak. A few broken bones is all. He'll make it. Oh and Schuler wanted to let me know that you are not to make a statement to the media after this is done. What happened was, Mr. Everley reportedly attacked some members of the Entertainment Department and engaged them in a fight. Injuries ensued."

"That's a load of bullshit!" Raquel screamed, "I was there! The guys went after Virgil for his money and then came after me!"

"I'm afraid that's not what I heard and neither will the media."

"But it's not true!"

Krystal looked over at Raquel and laughed, "Since when did the media care what was *true*?"

She walked over to her dressing table, "So Serena what do you plan on doing with Miss Polanski here since seems to be without a tour guide? No doubt, take her under your wing to score big with Schuler, eh?"

Serena looked over at her, "Shut up!" And then quickly turned to Raquel thinking, *Uh-oh, I have to actually, like, be kind to someone.* *Sigh* "Krystal's pulling your leg." And then with a smile way too big to genuine, "I'm really one of the nicest people here and we're going to have lots and lots of fun together! Okay?"

Raquel was a bit freaked our by the mood swing but it was her ticket out of the Public Relations office and she didn't want to stay in here any longer. "Sure."

"Alrighty then! We're off! See ya Krystal!" Serena had grabbed Raquel's arm and was just then leading her out of the office.

"Bye sweetheart. Take care." Krystal called as they left, sitting at her dressing table. It was at that moment that Raquel caught her last glimpse of Krystal Stephana putting on her flesh mask. It was rather, eerie staring at that face in the mirror, thinking about what truly lay underneath.

The outside hallway was still one big pile of papers. Unlabeled dramas and screenplays lay scattered, mixed, and rather crumpled up. Raquel made a mental note of how in the Theatre Department, everyone was dressed individually rather than the 'uniform' looks of the Entertainment and Social Department. Some wore different fruity-colored shorts; others wore an eccentric array of hats ranging from top hats, pith helmets, bowlers, turbans etc. Some people wore Hawaiian-typical-tourist button downs, others wore workout shorts and one guy even wore a trench coat. It was quite sight for someone who had been through several conformist departments, clothes-wise at least.

Serena was giving a full lecture on the Theatre Department: "So they started the Theatre Department for more revenue and whatnot. Most of these authors will send their screenplays to Hollywood and some of the more drama-oriented guys make it to Broadway. There's also a few guys who do the opera Libretti which is pretty cool." And then as if some random instinct over came her she turned to Raquel.

"AndI'mjustthenicest,sweetestpersonyou'veever metinthisplace,isn'tthatright?" saying it so fast that her sentence melted into one great big word.

"Sure…" Raquel started.

"Oh I forgot to mention that these guys ignore people who aren't in their department."

To give an example Serena approached an open office doorway and called to a young man who was sitting at a desk typing away furiously on his typewriter. "Excuse me handsome but could you help me. I've lost my way." The man didn't as much so much glance at Serena. He just continued typing away.

Serena grabbed Raquel and then led her to a spot where two girls were chatting. She started to tap furiously on one of the girls' shoulders shouting, "HEY! EXCUSE ME? EXCUSE ME?!!!" But the girls continued talking completely negligent of Serena's shouting. It was wondrous, watching people completely ignore you but who would gladly talk to everyone else around them.

"Why are they like that?" Raquel noticed the ignorant writers.

"Because," Serena whispered quietly (not that anyone would hear her), "Apparently most of these writer's are also big actors and they have, like this what they call 'actors' instinct'. It's something where any actor can sense who else is an actor and they won't talk to you unless you're an inducted actor." She looked around as if searching for someone. "And you can only be inducted by the department head."

"Who's that?

"Oh look, I see him. Right over there!"

They focused their attention in on a lanky, skinny man that Serena kept pointing to. He seemed to be a bit more aware of his surroundings and noticed the two girls.The man started to make his way towards them. He spoke first, "Allou. Can I 'elp zou?"

"Yes sir, this is Ms. Raquel Polanski and she's a new writer here and she was simply looking at the different Departments." Serena ushered Raquel in front of her.

"*Mademoiselle* Polanski, eet ees an 'onor to meet zumone weet ze courage dat you 'ave at zour age. My name es *Pierre Snooté*. We here at ze Theatre Deepartment, welcome zou, weet open arums!" He had grabbed Raquel's hand and lifted it to his lips for a small kiss. "But first! Zou must go through ze simulator!"

"No thank you Mr. Snooté, I was just looking.."

"Oh, do not be ridiculous! I inseest!" He then proceeded to put Raquel onto a small stage that was located in the middle of the hallway, wedged between two of the offices. Before she knew it Raquel was standing on the small stage and all the lights in the hallway had been shut off except for two spotlights that had been honed in on Raquel. The lights completely blinded her. "Zomeone get me zee goat!" Within a few seconds a random goat on a leash had appeared on stage alongside Raquel who was completely and utterly confused.

"Alright Mme. Polanski. You will perform improv weet zees goat. If zou pull off a zuckessful peyformánce, zou zhell bee part of zee Theatre Department!"

Raquel was still confused. She had no desire to be a part of the Theatre Department or to perform in front of perfectly good strangers. "Mr. Snooté I'm not trying to be a part of your department..."

"Ztarteeng in tree…:

"Really I'm not that interested…"

"…two…"

"Um..can I leave?"

"…one…"

"What's with the goat?"

"GO!"   Pierre yelled into a small mega phone.

Everything was silent for a few moments. Nobody spoke. Raquel just continued to stare like a deer in headlights, at the blinding stagelights. "Um.,."

"CUT!" It was Pierre. "*Mon dieu!* Zat was horrible! It lacked pazzhun and weet. I 'ave never zeen   zuch awful acting. Zou are dismissed!" The lights were turned off and everyone returned to their normal day routine, acting like Raquel didn't even exist. She had never acted in front of such a large group of people and did not see who Pierre was to judge somebody.

"Hey mister!" She yelled but Mr. Snooté had continued with the rest of the people to ignore the outsiders. "Hey Mr. Snooté, why don't you face me like a man? Hey, I'M TALKING TO YOU!"   But still nobody seemed to heed Raquel's presence. She kept screaming, "Come back here! Why doesn't anybody listening to me?! How snobby can you guys be?!"

Serena walked up to the upset Raquel. "It's okay sweetie." She said with her over-sized grin. "It's just how they've become wired. Their department has taught them to think a certain way. Almost like it's ingrained in their brains and they can't help it."

Raquel still felt awful. "Alright, let's get out of here."

"Sure thing."

It was so bad here. At least in the other departments, even though they treated you so terribly, they at least *acknowledged* you. Here no one didn't even so much as glance at you. To them you were insignificant. Your voice, your body, your opinions, your thoughts didn't matter. They had been taught 'what I know is best'.

Serena was just then leading Raquel back into the *Pacifier* which had been transformed. The DJ's mixing station was gone, the tables were gone, and the only person in the room was a lone janitor who was mopping the floor.

"And now we'll be going to the How-To Department where all sort of manuals are published by Ironwood Press."

Suddenly Raquel couldn't take it anymore: the people ignoring her, the fakeness of it all, and just how deplorable it all was. "Listen, Serena, I really don't think that I want to continue touring anymore."

Uh-oh, there goes my chance. Serena couldn't let this opportunity slip through her fingers. "What do you mean? Aren't you really enjoying your time with *me*?"

"No, in truth I'm not. In fact I'm really tired of all the lies you guys say and do. In fact I'm tired of everything here. I just don't like the way things are. I feel like they need to change." Her tone wasn't arrogant but more authoritative, passionate.

Suddenly Serena turned around. "You ungrateful little bitch. I try and be nice to you, lead you around, give you a tour for Christ's sakes and you are so ungrateful!"

"That's not what I mean. I just can't stand everything here. Having to falsify yourself in order for others to accept you, using your social positions for your own good; it's just so disgusting"

"Well that's just how things *are*. They're not going to change anytime soon. That's how *it's* always been and how *it's* always will be! And if you can't just deal with it I say you just get the hell out of here! Serena proceeded to then walk away from Raquel but she didn't heed the yellow 'CAUTION, WET' sign that had been placed across the dance floor by the janitor. It only took a few seconds before Serena's legs had come out from under her and thrown her up into the air. She landed on her back with a giant *THUD!*

Several paramedics loaded Serena Centre onto the stretcher.

"When and where were you born?"

"aAAARRRGooooooooooo!"

Serena Centre moaned from her position on the stretcher.

177

"She must've hit her head pretty hard." The paramedic looked at Raquel. "It seems like she may be a bit dazed for a little bit. Mild concussion, nothing more."

It had been the janitor who had ran to the nearest emergency telephone located in the corner of the room and rung up 911 in order to get paramedics to the scene. He then promptly disappeared.

Serena moaned again.

"There there dear, it'll be all right." One of the female paramedics soothed Serena with her voice and grabbed the stretcher along with a fellow EMT. The marched over to the elevator with the others following en suite. And once again Raquel found herself all alone.

She figured that she was just as lost as before. All she had done earlier was gone down to the sixth floor where she ended up in *The Pacifier* where the whole Serena Centre mess had occurred. It would just be wise to finish the tour and stick out this horrible excursion into what seemed like the depths of hell. She located the emergency telephone in the corner and then looked up the number for Schuler's office and then rang up the number. It was hard to believe that she was actually calling up a man she hated so much; who stood for so much that she thought was wrong.

*   *   *

Ch. 14

"Hello Schuler."

"Sam? Is that you?"

"Yep."

"Oh thank god. How's the hunt?"

"Well our Ms. Polanski is certainly taking the bait. It was a pain in the ass figuring someone who'd get her attention…"

"You used an email?"

"Yep."

"What did you do?"

"I prenteded ta be an ex. Name was Christian Huck."

"That seems good, very good."*slight breath*"Are you in private again?"

"Well if ya think a phone booth's pretty private…"

"What?! You're out in public?"

"Ey, take it easy Sully. Don't get your panties in a wad. Of course I'm careful."

deep breath"I guess it's okay. I will see you soon."

"Oh and Schuler, I really hope this doesn't turn out like the Johnston case…"

"I'm sorry but I had no way of knowing he was an NRA member…"

"Sully, that man could've kept fightin' till midnight with the shit he had stored in his house."

"I thought it was your job to figure out about the targets…"

"Yeah, but *basic* info is really appreciated…Why the hell am I even talking ta ya like this, I got like 30 seconds left. Just meet me tonight at exactly 7:00pm in the *Hawke* building and I'll bring her in for ya. I have no clue why ya want her alive but I'll deliver the goodies, I swear…" *line drops dead*

Schuler was shaking. *The sooner I get this over with the better everything will be…The sooner I get this over with the better everything will be...The sooner I get this over with the better everything will be...*

*   *   *

Michael Foster/The How-To Department

Secretary: "Hello, Mr. Schuler's office. How can I help ya?"

Raquel: "Hello? It's Raquel Polanski and I was wondering if I could be put through to Mr. Schuler at the moment?"

Secretary: "One moment."

(During which is an interlude of an awful attempt at Victorian-style music plays over poor audio with the occasional: "Thank you for your time. If you continue to hold, one of our representatives will be with you in a moment." messages that pop up at infrequent intervals.)

Schuler: "Hello?"

Raquel: "Hello Mr. Schuler, it's Raquel. There's been a terrible accident with my tour guide.

Schuler: "Oh yes I know; it's unfortunate about the boy.

Raquel: "Not him sir, it was a girl."

Schuler: "Mr. Everley was androgynous?!"

Raquel: "No, no, no. I mean I got a new tour guide, named Serena."

Schuler: "Oh, very well, I see. Yes I think Mrs. Penny mentioned something about you and Ms. Centre earlier. I will see to it that you have a new tour guide soon. I do hope you are enjoying yourself and have found a suitable department to join."

Raquel: "Somewhat…"

Schuler: "Oh, please hold a second."*barely audible whisper*"Please get me Mr. Foster from the Entertainment Department ASAP. We have a lone writer on floor six."*speaking up again*"Ms. Polanski, I have arranged for someone to meet you on the fifth floor. Please proceed to the closest elevator and then report to the fifth floor. You should encounter a Mr. Michael Foster."

Raquel: "Thank you."

Schuler: "No problem, please enjoy the rest of your tour!"

She hung up the phone and made her way to the elevator through the empty room. It looked so bleak compared to earlier. There were no longer any sweaty bodies, or junk food, or multi-chromed tiles, and the pretty awesome DJ had gone. Even the janitor had gone.

The fifth floor was built like many of the departments, as a series of halls. The walls were now a perfectly plain white and each and every office lacked a door. There was the same constant buzz of that the previous departments only it was much more organized. And people actually acknowledged you.

One of the employees carrying a bulky manuscript even bothered to say "Excuse me." To Raquel who then quickly granted his request. Another fabulous feature was that most of the faces were the same. Every man in the office wore glasses along with a series of adult braces and pimple-laden faces, as if puberty was still aflame in these young men. There was a bit of individualism with the daily outfit which consisted of plaid button downs, tucked into a vast array of khaki pants.

Raquel could not help but marvel at the series of bookshelves that lined the walls and boasted every single kind of manual thinkable. There were no pieces of fiction, no coloring books, no magazines, just manuals. There were manuals for cooking, cleaning, pet care, car care, financial advice, agricultural advice, magic tricks, pyramid schemes, and how to open off shore accounts without getting caught. The titles were another peculiarity which included everything from *Avoiding Udder Disaster: Making Sure Your Bovine is Happy* to *Apocalypse Now: In the Likely Event of a Zombie Outbreak*.

It was marvelous and so much better than all the previous departments.

Raquel happened to notice a mid-aged man who was approaching her with his hand extended. "Hi, you must be Raquel Polanski. Name's Michael Foster and I'm yer new tour guide."

Raquel shook his hand and smiled back. "It's a pleasure Mr. Foster."

"As it is mine. What'll you say we start gettin' the move on with this here tour? Any questions so far?"

Though her introduction to Mr. Foster had been rather brief and she hardly knew the guy, she couldn't help but wonder aloud, "What is this place?"

"Oh this here is the little ole' How-To Department of Ironwood Press. These guys make all those fancy-smancy manuals that Ironwood Press publishes and distributes worldwide. They're also the sworn enemies of the Entertainment Department." He stopped walking and just shook his head at the whole prospect.

"Why's it gotta be like that? I mean no one said they had to be enemies." Raquel looked up inquiringly at Mr. Foster.

"I 'spose that's the way it's always been. Nobody from the Entertainment Department is 'spose to associate with anybody from the How-To Department."

"But does it really have to be like that? Couldn't you just give up your differences and get along? It's kind of stupid if you ask me."

Michael looked over at her and laughed softly, "I guess things don't always have to be this way but that's how they've always been and folks here don't take too kindly to change around these parts, Miss Polanski."

She sighed and the continued their walk throughout the long hallway. Raquel noticed one office in particular where people came in went like flies. It was the busiest by far. "Who's in there?" She pointed.

"There? Why that would be the department head. I.Q. what's his face. Apparently a big wig when it comes to writing manuals."

There was a sudden nasally shriek in the air, "Oh my goodness, it's someone from the Entertainment Department!" One of the pimple-faced writers had just noticed Michael.

Within seconds the whole scene turned hectic. People dropped their manuscripts and started to swarm Raquel and her guide screaming things like:

"Give us the bonehead!"

"We want the tough guy!"

"Down with the Entertainment Department!"

Michael only laughed as he watched the oncoming crowd form, "C'mon, I'll take all y'all little punks!" This statement only made some of the writers continue to rage on and press closer and closer to Michael and Raquel, forcing them up against the wall.

Raquel screamed and Michael started to crack his knuckles for one big free for all when a nasally voice rang throughout the crowd. "SILENCE!"

Just like that, the entire crowd was silenced against their will. From somewhere towards the very back of the mob people started to part as a voice made its way closer and closer to the two victims. "I will be the judge of what to do with this alleged Entertainee." The same nasally voice pronounced as it parted more and more people until the crowd opened up right before Raquel stood a man much smaller than she was.

"Ah what do we have here?" The little man eyed Raquel and her guide. "A young girl and an Entertainee. How very interesting…"

"And just who might you be?" Raquel looked down at the little man.

The guy looked thoroughly insulted. "You mean you don't recognize me? *Moi?*"

"Um…no. Should I?"

"Why girl I am the world-renowned, award-winning, Irwin Quincy Highly. The author of various manuals: I.Q. Highly!" He was now facing heaven-ward with an arm stretched in the same direction, looking like some Shakespearean character in existential throes.

Raquel only shook her head. "No, can't say I've ever heard of you."

"You mean you haven't heard of any of my work?! *Shit Happens: Removing Bowel Stains from Your Carpet*, *More Bang for Your Buck: Homemade Firecrackers, A Bigger You in 30 Minutes: Do it Yourself Breast Implants?*"

Raquel couldn't help but ponder over the safety of the last title. Again she shook her head.

"My god! How are children raised these days?" Highly took one more look at the odd couple and asked, "Well explain the reason you're with this Entertainee simpleton, huh?"

"I'm her tour guide ya idiot. We just happened to be comin' through here peacefully when one of your little punks happened to scream at me and this happened." Michael motioned towards the crowd.

"I'll have you know Mr. Foster, that my little 'punks' were right in doing so. You know that in the Jassol-Highly pact of '08 that we are not allowed in your department and vice versa…"

"Unless there is an emergency or there is a tour going on. Forgot that Mr. High Horse, now didn't you?"

Highly tuned bright purple, "How dare you call me by such an idiotic nickname…the proper title is I.Q. Highly. Mr. Schuler will make you pay for your insolence!"

Michael only laughed, "Make sure he pays for your acme removal too!"

I.Q. snapped "GET THEM!" He pointed with a long ugly finger at Raquel and Michael. There was a sudden surge in pressure as the crowd closed in on the trapped couple. Michael used his fist in one great big swoop that knocked over a great many How-To writers who took their fellow companions down with them as well. Michael grabbed Raquel and swung her over his shoulder and carried her out from the mob of angry writers. The entrance to the elevator was blocked and Michael had to pummel his way through before he managed to knock down one of the bookshelves, scattering manuals across the floor.

"Our manuals!" Someone shrieked. The fallen shelf cut off the crowd from the area nearest the elevator. All the writers just looked over at Michael and Raquel who found their way into the elevator, unstoppable only due to all the little manual-authors' wimpiness.

*   *   *

"Sonofabitch." Kyle Williams (no relationship to Colin), FBI Agent sat with his partner Agent James Rivers as they surveyed the *Hawke* building from their 1987 Back SS El Camino with dark tinted windows, which just so happened to be the exact same car that hit man Schiano drove as well. "We track this guy for three months and what do we get? Not a single damn thing!" Both Rivers and Williams had been tracking a certain hit man, Samuel Schiano, who had been notorious for collaborating with various corporations in taking out "certain nuisances". The Federal Government had first learned about Schiano after a series of deaths in Beverley Hills were said to be linked to a man known only to his clientele as "Sam". And now they had been hot on his tail every since his most recent "job" in Santa Fe where the old assassin had gotten sloppy and left evidence against himself.

The two agents had needed the Schiano case in order to redeem themselves from the terrible "Harrison Incident". The previous summer, Special Agents Kyle Williams and James Rivers had been involved with Special Agent in Charge

Alexander Harrison. Agent Harrison had decided to round up drug dealer Whitey Rodriguez in a Southern Californian warehouse. Harrison accidently forgot to inform the two of the trap and set Williams and Rivers to clean up the streets of drug dealers and prostitution rings. Fortunately both of the agents noticed the face of Whitey Rodriguez strolling across the town on his way to what they presumed to be a drug deal. The two stalked after the notorious Mafioso and found themselves in a warehouse that Rodriguez & co. had strolled into. A major shoot-out ensued where Rodriguez escaped unscathed and Special Agent in Charge Harrison was not pleased with the two dimwits' decisions. Both had nearly been suspended before Harrison sent them off on a case dealing with an odd assassin, which had driven them clear across the country.

Well, they *had* been on his trail at least. Now it seemed cold. "I swear that he said over the phone to meet at 7:00 pm at the *Hawke* building where he would meet Schuler." Rivers had self-appointed himself as audio recorder/interpreter and he just so happened to have placed a bug right in a phone booth that Schiano would use.

"We just don't know what girl they were talking about…"

"Aww shit…we got a potential victim and we can't even locate her or Schiano. Well we're just SOL then, ain't we pal?"

"You're attitude's not helping any, you little bastard…Why don't you shove it already?"

"Up yours…"

"Hey cool it, or I'll take you out and use your ass for hit man-bait. How's that sound?"

"Sounds pretty damn fine with me, seeing that we're probably not going to find him…"

"How about this Williams: we get out of the car, split up and I can take the back of the building and you'll monitor the front…"

"That could be dangerous…"

"Oh yeah you're right, real dangerous. We can't get hurt you know."

"Nope."

"You know what, it's probably a bunch of sick little kids calling each other and playing Mafia."

"Yeahhh."

"I don't know, but I think we can leave now…"

Rivers slowly began to turn the key in the ignition.

"HOLY SHIT! IT"S THE GIRL!" Williams had suddenly cried out.

"Good god kid, keep your pants on. There's plenty of girls back home…"

"No you dipshit, I mean she's *THE* girl!"

"I know how it is: young kid sees some girl and believes it's love at first sight. Don't you get married on that basis, they'll divorce you faster than you can say…"

Williams suddenly sank his hands into Rivers' face and turned his head around. Sure enough a young girl, wrapped in a thick, dark coat was standing alongside the pavement.

"Wait…Schiano said something about a girl and…OH MY GOD IT'S HER!!!!!"

Rivers gunned the car and thunderous roar broke out.

Williams spat out another round of obscenities.

*   *   *

The Erotica Department/Alison Evensen

Raquel was panting heavily along with Michael who had suggested that they see the next floor after what they had just witnessed.

"What department could this be?"

"Oh you'll see…" there was a sort of mischievous twinkle to his eye.

The elevator door opened and Raquel stepped into a dimly lit hallway. Sexy sounding slow jams played over a sound system. No one could be seen in the hallway. Michael wheezed, "Well it's not all that bad in here. Just kind of dark…hold on. Let me get a breather,"*huff*"Man that stuff really…really takes your breath away." Raquel put out a hand to steady herself against one of the walls. She looked up with horror to realize that her hand was placed directly between a pair of breasts that belonged to a Victoria's Secret model who stretched across a poster that had been pinned up to the wall. Raquel recoiled her hand in terror and cried, "What is this place?!"

"Welcome to the Erotica Department baby." A sly voice had answered from one of the office doorways where a young man stood with a button down shirt that was opened all the way and a pair of pants that were pulled a little low.

"Oh…" Raquel only looked at the eye candy but Michael became defensive.

"Git, ya creep." The discouraged man went back into his office shutting the door that had a sign stating: **DATE, MATE, BREAK UP, REPEAT**.

"I don't like this place very much…" Raquel shuddered at the words on the sign.

"Not very many folks in their right minds do, Miss Polanski. But you'd be surprised how much money this all brings in; the amount of money people spend to get a sick sort of thrill."

Michael shook his head in an almost sad manner and sighed a little.

"Hey Mikey baby, how 'bout you come into my office so we can have a little 'chat'." A brunette woman was wearing nothing but her undergarments and a pink silk bathrobe that allowed for a decent amount of cleavage to be shown.

"No thanks Charlene." Michael just walked past her and the foxy women retreated into her den. Raquel noticed that it took all his might not to just turn and look at her.

"Do I want to know?"

"Ex, used to work up in Entertainment and then some low life seduced her down here, broke her heart and she's stayed ever since."

"Oh, I'm sorry."

"Don't be, I should've never let her go. Never was it more true in my life, the whole 'you don't know what ya got 'til it's gone' thing."

They continued to walk on in silence until they came to small office located in the very corner which stood out from the rest. The posters of scantily-clad women had been torn off the walls around the door that read: **A son Ev nsen R man e De art nt** across the door. Compared to the other doors the paint was a bit more faded and some letters were even missing.

"Now this is one smart girl here." Michael motioned to the door. "She's about 22 and she's got several bestsellers under her belt already; just phenomenal. Only she's losing readers to these here other folks. Most people are out for a cheap thrill."

He politely knocked on the door.

"Hello?"

"It's Michael, Alie."

"Hey, come in!" The voice sounded welcoming compared to everyone else Raquel had talked to.

They let themselves in to find a young girl sitting at her desk with a half-eaten sandwich in one hand and another hand that was typing away on a small desktop.

She smiled at her visitors, "Hey Mike, what's up?"

"Not much Alie, just showing this here girl around the office, giving an orientation. Name's Raquel Polanski."

Alison offered a soft hand to Raquel who shook it rather gladly. "Man, I didn't think you'd be brave enough to bring someone around here, especially a new comer to this place. You tryin' to scare her off?" She teased.

Michael only smiled, "I had to bring her to you. You're probably one of the smartest people I know."

"Aw shucks Mike, you praise people too much." Alison set her sandwich down and wiped at a few crumbs left by her mouth. "Please have a seat."

Raquel and Michael sat down and Alison started off the conversation, "Any questions about the job or how things work?" She had directed it towards Raquel.

"Not really anything off the top of my head, but why does your window outside look faded? I guess that it use to say 'Romance Department' at one time or another?"

Alison sighed. "There was once a Romance Department that I was part of but then in '010 Schuler decided that Romance was in no way *stimulating* enough for readers. So he changed it to 'The Erotica Department' at which time most of the young romance writers left and joined the Miscellaneous Department. But I stayed."

"Why?"

Alison looked up thoughtfully, "Because I thought I could become a sort of 'light' to other writers here. Those things out there, that's not love." She paused to consider her words, "That's sex. I mean, do you love someone because you need them? Or do you need them because you love them?"

Raquel and Michael looked a bit confused.

"Ugh. You guys know: in other words do we fall in love with other people for what they can do, or rather, for what they are?" I mean isn't that the whole point of falling in love?"

She looked a bit exasperated but Raquel started to grip what she was saying.

"We fall in love with a *person* rather than a *thing*. I think that's why so many relationships fail. It's because we often fall in love with something a person can do for us (that 'need' they fulfill); whether it may be protection, financial security, an increase in social standing, or sexual fulfillment. It's natural for us as human beings to desire those things, but they shouldn't get in the way of actually being able to love somebody. When you fall in love, *truly* in love I mean, you fall in love with another person: the good, the bad, and the ugly. When we truly love someone it's unconditional; there's no catch to it. I believe that you can say that you love someone when you have seen them at their worst and can still say, "I love them." No one ever said it was gonna be easy, but true love is worth it."

It was then that Raquel actually felt *good* about something someone had said at the offices all day. .

"Wow Alison, that's…really great." Raquel smiled.

"Thanks. I've tried to get that point across with my co-workers but they are still too focused on things that don't matter. But I pray and hope that one day they'll actually open their eyes and feel that they have this hollow, empty love for peoples' abilities and will start to love people where it counts, on the inside."

And that was the first time that day that Raquel felt a spark of hope.

*   *   *

The sound of a car engine gunning sent Raquel into a sprint. She saw the Black El Camino just up the road and remembered it from earlier in the day, when she and Christian had stopped by the park and now he was here...*Oh no, oh no, I thought it'd be him, I thought, no*...She began running like never before. She hadn't cared about twisting her ankle in stilettos. Raquel looked around for the safest place to hide. *There! That alley. They'll never see me there.*

"Damn it, why is she running into the alley? Doesn't she know that's the worst place to..." Williams was shouting his head off in the car.

"Roll yer window down and shout at her that if she wants to live, *not* to go into the alley!"

Williams stuck his torso out of the window and began to quote Rivers verbatim while flailing his arms.

Raquel could only hear "Don't go in the alley if you want to live!" *They're threatening a chase.*

Better than giving up now. Raquel quickly turned and hid in the darkness.

"'Cuse me ma'am?"

She jumped only to find a hobo standing behind her with his palms outstretched. "Got some change you could spare an ol' soul like me this New Year's Day?" He smiled.

"I'm in a bit of a pinch right now…"

"So am I. See, I'm looking for this girl," the hobo grinned, "named Raquel Polanski; you wouldn't happen to know her would you?"

Raquel could hardly speak before a prickly hand had shot up a strange-colored handkerchief and that covered her nostrils. Raquel Polanski could hardly understand why the New York Evening had become sans soleil.

*   *   *

*Lunch Break/The Terribly Cliché Workshops of
Professor Ali Redi Dunne/Ultima Cuarto*

Michael and Raquel had quickly exited the Erotica Department and were now on their way to the lobby.

"Why the lobby? I've already seen it." Raquel looked inquiringly at Michael.

"Because it's my lunch break which is above all else."

"You can't be serious…"

"Oh I'm quite serious sugar pie. I need me some lunch before we can proceed with this here tour."

"But you can't!" She was starting to get stubborn.

"Oh yes I can. Watch me."

The elevator doors opened and Michael fumbled out and started to pace across the Ironwood Press lobby towards where the cafeteria was located.

"Fine. Go on! Leave me for some food fatass!"

But he didn't so much as bat a lash at her and continued to trek towards the lunch Mecca. She looked around. Now she was really screwed. She hadn't even finished the tour yet with two more departments to visit. Raquel decided to look around the lobby until she could find someone willing enough to take her to the last two departments.

The lobby was mostly empty except for the cafeteria and a hallway that branched off the main foyer that contained several "mini-auditoriums" as the writers like to refer to them as. Raquel couldn't help but notice a giant white sign that stood by one of the MA's set of entrance doors that read: **Suffering from writer's block?! Need a quick book?! Look no further! Professor Ali Redi Dunn has come with his 'mystical equation' for the perfect book that will land your book on bestseller lists, guaranteed!*** And in smaller print from the asterisk read: *unless of course your writing sucks, which is, in any case, *your* fault. *Sounds interesting, maybe I'll find someone in hear who'd make a worthy tour guide.*

She tried to enter the room as subtlety as she could but still a few heads turned and then turned back to face the Professor who was pacing back and forth on the stage saying an unstoppable soliloquy, "...make sure that the romantic couple is good looking and comes together through some dangerous situation..."

207

Raquel took a seat in the back by a young doe-eyed blonde guy who was scribbling notes on a small notepad. He looked up and smiled with a quiet, "Hi."

"Hi." Raquel answered. "Raquel Polanski. You?" She was being rather hasty about proper greetings but she didn't have time given the circumstances.

"Irving Quinn Lowly, or better known as I.Q. Lowly."

Raquel had indeed heard of I.Q. Lowly. His novels were always the kind that were on sale at the grocery stores and could be found in hotel rooms across the country.

"...must engage the characters in at least two well-written sex scene, which never ceases to fascinate readers..."

"Yeah, I've seen your books around."

"Great, I'm glad to meet a fan."

Raquel would not have gone so far as to say *fan*. She'd talk to a good friend back home who'd said that his novels were all the *same* thing just with a slightly different plot and a title change.

"…there should always be lots of violence and explosion…"

"So who's this guy?" Raquel had motioned towards Prof. Dunn.

"Oh he's great," Lowly began. "I always come to this guy's workshops and let me tell you they are *amazing*."

The word *always* struck her.

"…if you appeal to someone's need to be stimulated, he will continue to buy you novels again and again…"

"So he just teaches the same plots, but in different arrangements?"

"Yeah pretty much., but I've always used the mystical arrangement myself and it never fails."

Never, *always*, it was all the same.

"…and that is how you will manage to get your books into grocery stores, book clubs, and hotel shelves successfully. Thank you for being attentive throughout this lecture ladies and gentlemen, I hope you enjoyed our time together as much as I did!"

There was a loud applause and soon Raquel found that I.Q. Lowly didn't have a long enough attention span. After the applause died down and Prof. Dunn left the stage writers began getting up from seats and walking off to the exit. "Excuse me, Mr. Lowly?"

"Yes?"

"I was wondering if you could possibly help me find a tour guide. You see, I'm a new writer here and I was almost about to tour the last two departments here until I was so rudely abandoned by my tour guide."

Lowly laughed, "Oh please don't look at me ma'am. I'm very busy and I don't think I'd make a good tour guide at all, but that woman over there might be able to help you." He pointed to a small cluster of writers and one woman in particular who stood out. She was not young; her hair was a pure snow-white and had been tied up in a bun. "That's Mrs. Cuarto from the Miscellaneous Department. She's one of the senior editors and probably one of the oldest people in the company."

Raquel made a quick nod to Lowly thanking him for his advice and then she proceeded to approach Mrs. Cuarto.

She was hesitant at first but she finally summoned the courage to pipe up a small, "Excuse me, Mrs. Cuarto?"

"Yes?" The woman turned to face Raquel. Her face was ancient; canyons of wrinkles that much experience brings had formed around her fierce dark brown eyes. The woman certainly had some years on herself but she held herself erect.

"I hope I didn't interrupt anything…"

"Of course not, child." The Hispanic woman smiled down at her. "In what way can I help you?"

"Well…you see…I had this tour guide who…bailed…and…"

"Say no more child. From what point did your tour end?"

"We had just passed the fourth floor and…"

"Ah the dreaded fourth floor. I see. So you think you are prepared for the third floor?"

"Um... I don't know what's on the third floor?"

"Speak no more. I shall take you there child." She turned then to the other writers she had been speaking to. "Excuse me children, but this child is in need of some knowledge which I shall gladly give her." Ultima then turned to Raquel and beckoned with a finger. "Come."

Raquel chatted with Ultima a little bit on their way to the elevator and found out some interesting things. That Ultima had come from Mexico as just a small child to the Big Apple where she decided to live for the rest of her life, that she didn't know Spanish, that she was an editor in the Miscellaneous Department, that she was retiring in May and as was ritual for retiring employees, and she was to give farewell speech that would take place in Mid-December.

"I really hope I'm not keeping you from it..."

"Nonsense! It'll start in an hour, plenty of time to tour the last two departments."

Raquel hopped into the elevator alongside Ultima.

"So what's on the third floor?"

"The Burn Out Department."

"Is it as bad as the Erotica Department?" Raquel looked at Ultima with pleading eyes.

"No child, it's worse."

*　　*　　*

There was a strange sweet smell and the room appeared to be shaded in a light blue light. Raquel Polanski had awakened sitting upright on a chair, with her hands bound behind her. It took a second for her eyes to adjust to the light and turn the shadows into recognizable shapes. She realized that she was sitting in the Entertainment Department. The city lights of New York shimmered through the glass causing the whole room to illuminate a blue tint to everything, intermingled with the shadows of snowflakes. Raquel could not scream, in fact she didn't know what to think of her dilemma. *You're so stupid.*

"I'm finally glad you're awake," a familiar face called out from the shadows. "I finally wanted to talk face-to-face with you." Mitchell Schuler slowly emerged from the shadows dragging a chair behind him and a large stack of papers bundled underneath his left armpit. The shiny glint off the barrel of a gun betrayed its location upon his hip. *My manuscript…*"As you can see I've been looking forward to something like this for quite awhile and I can't wait for our little chat!"

Raquel only scowled at him. "You dirty bastard."

"You think hurling insults at me will set you free? Do you think by degrading me you can save yourself? Why you're pathetic as everyone else." Schuler was now perfectly seated with the manuscript displayed on his lap.

Raquel was quickly hushed. From somewhere in the shadows she could hear the light tapping of boots as someone else paced back and forth. "What do you want from me Schuler?"

The old man let out a chortle, "That's a loaded question Ms. Polanski, but I guess you could say it boils down to, your life."

"Why would you say something like that?"

"Well you see Ms. Polanski," he motioned to the manuscript, "When I first read this I was so…so touched by it, that it reminded me, in fact, or an event that occurred quite some time ago. Yes upon a clear and starry night…"

"What was it?" Raquel looked generally curious now.

"It was the night I murdered Antonio Benjamin."

Time seemed to come to a standstill as Raquel tried to take in the news. "You mean he never…"

"Committed suicide? No. I helped that poor bastard to an early death. I'm just surprise I was never caught. However I couldn't help but feel that your novel so much alike that night. When I first began to read I found, to my astonishment, that the opening scene somehow encompassed the very feeling that one gets when murdering their superior. Of course, I am still a human being, such as yourself and I was moved by guilt. Yes absolutely ridden with it. At that time I decided I could no longer deal with the guilt again; I needed to destroy the source of my guilt." Schuler then began to pull the very first sheet of paper off of the manuscript and ripped it into a million shreds. "That source consisted of you and your story and now I shall see to it that they are both taken care of." He continued to rip another piece of paper from the manuscript.

Raquel cried out from her chair, "What are you doing? Stop!" Tears began to fall down her cheeks. Her cries persisted for several more

216

minutes but Schuler only continued to shred page after page of the manuscript. Finally she stopped sobbing, by now three quarters of the manuscript lie on the floor, in a mixture of paper mâché. "Why are you doing this?" She finally screamed aloud. Raquel found hard to find a gulp of air in between the sobs.

Schuler suddenly stopped shredding and looked straight into Raquel's face. "People are nasty animals, Ms. Polanski. They are selfish, and cruel, and needy, and wanting, and so very stupid. I don't know why you are shocked now Ms. Polanski. After all, you live in a very unjust world, one that seeks to subject you to its ways. You live a world that shall see to your dying day that you Raquel Polanski, behaved in fashion with how everybody perceived you and that you abided by what others thought. Nobody cares who you really are Ms. Polanski. Nobody cares. You may somehow believe you can change things, well you can't. The world as we know it now has been the world as it always shall be, and there is nothing that a simple and foolish girl like you could ever possibly do to change it."

There was long pause before Raquel could muster up the courage to speak. "I don't believe you."

"What?"

"Maybe you are right Mr. Schuler, maybe nobody does care. Maybe the whole world is really a terrible place: one that doesn't care for me and simply seeks to use me. Maybe I really won't have mattered anything in the existence of the billions of other people. But I can tell you one thing, Mr. Schuler, *I cared.* I put my whole heart into the way I looked at things and decided I wasn't going to be just like the world; because we're called to be higher than that."

"Why would you care? After all, the only thing that happens to you in this life is you get used, people betray you, backstab you, and hate you. And here you are spouting nonsense about how much *you cared*. It's so syrupy it makes me sick. Naïve people like you are so sickening."

"No," her voice slowly rose, "Naivety is a state of being, optimism on the other hand is a choice. And I have made a choice of my own will. You see Mr. Schuler, if in fact what you say is true, than I had a heart that was *too* big. I poured out *too much* of it into other people. The funny thing is, I don't regret it. Because where everyone else walked around with some big gap in their chest, I had a heart that was two sizes too big, and I'll always wonder: could such a thing have ever been bad?".

"What lovely last words." Schuler was standing next to Raquel now and the cold steel of the gun's barrel was now pressed against her head.

And yet in those last few moments of her life Raquel Polanski was filled with a strange yet unwavering peace. She looked out at the fall of snowflakes along the giant widows, casting small shadows as the lightly fell out of her view. Something about their presence made things a bit more tolerable. They offered just the slightest bit of comfort. Raquel Polanski was now ready for whatever was to come.

He pulled the trigger.

*　　　*　　　*

The Burn Out Department

Ultima led Raquel into a room that resembled a mental institution. The walls and floor were

219

colored a dull white which was only illuminated by the bright florescent bulbs that covered the greater expanse of the ceiling. The room was barren except for a series of white benches that were pushed up against one wall and a pharmacy-esque counter on the opposite wall. Only a few people occupied the entire room. At the counter an elderly woman stood at attention. In front of her were two giant-sized stamps: one green, one red. Only a few nervous looking men and women sat at the benches clutching manuscripts. *What do the authors do here?* Raquel found herself curious to find out.

The old woman at the desk called out: "Number 231, Number 231, please report to the counter immediately."

A young woman with a dog-eared manuscript quickly approached the desk and started rambling almost incoherent nonsense about a book. Everyone could hear as the old woman cried out: "DENIED!"

She raised the giant red stamp and shoved brought down with full force on the manuscript. The young author cried as she quickly removed her manuscript and started to run towards the elevator, hoping for escape.

"What is this place?" Raquel was looking intently at Ultima.

"This is the Burn Out Department, my child. It's where the writers whose value has decreased to an all time low find themselves. Some are authors suffering of months of writer's block. Others are those, whom over the years have grown stale, have lost their passion for writing and left their talents to rot. Still others are writers who were simply called to devote more energy and time to their more emotional and personal lives rather than to their writing."

Ultima motioned Raquel to the direction of the benches. She pointed to young man, sharply dressed, with a very upright posture. "Ask him, child. Ask him how he ended up here." Raquel was hesitant but Ultima only nodded. "There is no reason to be afraid."

Raquel slowly walked up the young man who had noticed her long before she began to talk to him. A jumble of words rushed out, "Miss Cuarto wanted me to ask you…how did you…"

"End up here?" He smiled slightly.

"Ye…yes, if it wouldn't be too rude to ask."

"Oh, not at all. Here. Why don't you join me on the bench?" He picked up an old bundle of loose leaf papers and motioned for Raquel to sit. She quickly took a seat and listened to the young man begin:

"When I first began to work for Ironwood Press, I was part of the C.O.T.C Department, you know the one at the very top? Well I was a perfectionist in fact. All my t's were crossed, all my i's dotted. But one must know that perfection is impossible for any human to achieve. I suppose I liked to possess a sense of control with the things I created. We like the delusion that we can control more things than we actually can. Power and control are in fact, both delusions. But like everyone else, I got addicted to these delusions. And it just got worse and worse. Eventually I could not limit the confines of my job to just the workplace and soon I found that my work life had spilled into that of my emotional one. That's when the downward spiral hit. No new ideas. Writer's block is what happened to me. I lost my position in the department and sent to seek out other's assistance. But the block never lifted. I never got any better."

"This department was established by the company to take care of those who were the straying sheep, the weak links. They give you so many days to produce something that will say: 'see, I'm not completely worthless, I still got some talent in me.' It's like an employment death-sentence. Very few people can go throw the BOD and stay at the company. But see I know there is no hope for me. I have peace in knowing that there is not hope. I had to accept that fact that I can't write like I use to any longer. You see, I've come to terms with what I really am and that is worthless, but only to this company.

Raquel was shocked that he felt this way. "But aren't you afraid? For your job? For what you're going to do when you're unemployed?"

"I've thought about it. But you see, I've learned to find peace in what I do not know. Humans look for peace in all the wrong places. We seek it though control, through delusions, but perfection can only be brought so far. No, we need to find it in the unknown."

"Number 232, Number 232, please report to the front counter immediately."

"Looks like my turn's up." The young man slowly rose from the bench and grabbed his folder of papers. He slowly walked away towards the front counter. Raquel noticed that her wrist had just been clasped by Ultima's hand.

"I'm afraid the time requires that we leave now my child." And with that, Raquel and Ultima both marched back to the elevator, got in and waited for the doors to close. The very last thing Raquel ever saw in that elevator was that young man going up to the counter to receive his fate. But the doors closed. Raquel would probably never know what happened to that young man, or ever see him again. But something inside her, told her it was okay…

*   *   *

Or to be more precise, Christian Martinez had, aiming exactly 5 feet too high. The bullet soared over Schuler and Schiano's heads and lodged itself into the wall.

"Who the hell…"

Several more shots caused Schuler and the lowly assassin to duck for cover. The only lights that illuminated the room were the occasional shots being fired across the room. Raquel quickly slammed herself, full force into the ground, bringing down the chair along with her. The bonds broke and she quickly crawled away to hide underneath a desk. Bullets whizzed through the air and shattered pieces of furniture throughout the room. Raquel glanced towards the elevator. Both antagonists had made a chair-and-desk barrier not but a few yards from the elevator doors. *Shit*. She quickly crawled towards the opposite end of the room were the opposing gun fire had set in motion the series of events.

"Miss Polanski, don't fret! I shall free of us of this situation!" Raquel had never been gladder to hear Christian's voice.

"Christian! Christian! Help!"

"I've yet to find you yet Miss Polanski. I shall try as long as I can keep the enemy under fire. I regret that I never was a master of firearms."

On the opposite end of the room Sam Schiano had located the sound of Raquel's yelping. He fired two more shots in the general direction of Christian before turning to Schuler. "I'm goin' in for the girl."

"No, that was not the agreement!" Schuler hissed.

"I don't give a damn about our agreement any longer. We kill her, we lure the guy out. And once we have that idiot out in the open, my job's finished."

He tore off from the bunker and began advancing towards the rows of desks and chairs. Raquel slowly stopped dead in her tracks. The looming shadow of Sam Schiano was but a few feet from the desk she was curled under. Occasional outburst of pistol shots rang in the background. Schiano looked over to see a slight silhouette shift underneath one of the desks.

With the swiftness of a cat, Schiano leaped atop the desk. Raquel heard a quick *THUD!* And then saw the head of Sam Schiano, with a wide, obscene grin spread across it.

"Surprise!" Schiano manically laughed and slowly brought his pistol from above the table and leveled with her face. Two quick *BANG!*'s and suddenly Schiano seemed to slump off the table. His body lay on the ground while a dark crimson puddle began to form underneath it.

"She's mine you damn fool!" It was Schuler calling across the room. Satisfied that he'd shot the impudent assassin.

Raquel had nearly screamed and if that didn't make matters worse, the elevator doors began to open and a canister of tear gas was flung into the middle of the room.

"FBI, nobody move!"

Raquel was suddenly up and about trying to look for Christian. "Christian!" She screamed. "Christian!"

Williams and Rivers could hear the girl screaming. They were trying their best to locate her.

Raquel was now chocking on the air, as the thick gas stung her eyes and seemed to make the air heavier. She could suddenly see a silhouette walking in her general direction through the smoke. Raquel began to run towards it. *That has to be Christian!* Upon further examination, it proved otherwise. Mitchell Schuler was standing only 15 feet away. He raised his pistol.

Christian had just spotted Raquel through the smoke, only she was frozen; turned towards something. He then realized that it was Schuler and his pistol that was aimed carefully at Raquel. Christian let out a cry, "RAQUEL!"

In the expanse of 5 seconds there were two shots. Raquel could feel a puff of air, a sharp sting, and then she realized the coin-sized-scarlet-colored wounds that appeared on her torso. The last thing she would later recount seeing, was Schuler's body being riddled with bullets before the world went dark.

*   *   *

The Miscellaneous Department

Raquel was all alone with Ultima in the elevator.

"You have learned much today child, haven't you?" Ultima looked down at her with sympathetic eyes. "I am sorry but with every ounce of wisdom we acquire, there is also a slight bit of pain that tails it not far behind."

Raquel had been so stressed out by the entire day she couldn't bear to imagine what lay ahead.

"Are you ready to see one of the most interesting departments you shall see child?"

"It'd be nice for a change." Raquel let out a sigh.

The elevator opened and Raquel stepped into a department vastly different from all the others. The walls were splatter-painted in the most fabulous way. The carpet was composed of multiple patterns of carpet that had been seemingly stitched together. Here doors were open and authors conversed freely with one another. It wasn't chaotic, or busy, or unorganized, but *energetic*. Individualism was prevalent here like the Theatre Department but not so outrageous.

People's choice in clothes ranged from casual to formal, modest to revealing, sneakers to flip flops, stilettos to sandals. There was no universal haircut or uniform everyone simply had their own style.

Everyone who saw Raquel nodded and said, "Welcome" or "hi" or "how ya doin'?" Not within two minutes of taking it all in young man came running through the hall with a flip phone raised high above his head, pursued by another man who kept yelling, "Stop! Someone apprehend that vagrant!" The young man with the phone ran into the elevator closing the "shut door" button before the other man could reach the elevator. "Blast it!" The young man left shouted. "Mr. Wagner I will very well reprimand you! You shall not prevail!"

People laughed at the whole sight while Raquel couldn't help but be dumbfounded by the whole scene. She had just witnessed the famous Christian Martinez giving chase over a cell phone. She wanted very badly to talk to Mr. Martinez but he was soon on the next elevator.

Mrs. Cuarto turned to look at Raquel. "I'm afraid child, that I must go prepare for my speech child. Will you be okay by yourself?"

"I think so Ultima." Raquel smiled an actually reached out to hug her. "Thank you so much."

Ultima only smiled, "You deserved it child. Now, run along, please don't be shy, the authors here are extremely friendly.

Raquel had never encountered so many colorful characters within one hour than she had that day. The Misc. Department housed a variety of people from various walks of life including editors, agents and writers. People eagerly showed Raquel their manuscripts, illustrations, and offices. It was in that time that Raquel had become acquainted with multiple people: young children's author and illustrator Thomas Wallace, who had paintings and sketches hung up all about his office; Emily Stamboli, the woman known famous for her memoir about farm life. There was Brie Houston, a transfer author from Gold Canyon Publishers with seemingly boundless energy. There was Leila Giovanni, the poet and avid F. Scott Fitzgerald enthusiast. There was also Cristina Muñez, an agent whom personally oversaw most of the writers in the Misc. Department. And finally there was Sierra Lichtenstein, the Puerto Rican-German immigrant who was the personal secretary to Mr. Martinez and spoke a very broken dialect of English.

"Is Mr. Martinez in yet?" Raquel popped her head into the abnormally sized office that had its own reception room were Ms. Lichtenstein stood filing her nails.

"No, Meester Martinze ees a steel AOL. He going to be back soon."

"Do you have any time when?"

"No, he gone 'cause Meester Vagner steel a hees *teléfono*."

"Oh can you please let me know when he gets back?"

"I weel try, but I canna promise any ting."

"Thanks."

"*Lo siento, señorita.*"

At that time the invisible voice came out of the PA system. "*Ladies and Gentlemen, we would please encourage you all to attend the farewell address of Mrs. Ultima Cuarto which*

232

will take place in the Miscellaneous Department's MA. The speech will begin in about twenty minutes. We hope to see you there."

Raquel decided to attend to see what a women like Ultima had to say and how she would go about saying it. She hardly knew the woman for about a few hours but had felt like they were very close.

The MA was located almost at the far end of the Miscellaneous Department's hallway. It was spacious and clean and by the time Raquel arrived but mostly full. And by the time the speech was beginning, new arrivals of people had to be shown in and made to stand against the walls ad from far away. About five minutes before hand, head editor walked out on stage and gave a brief introductory speech about Mrs. Cuarto and all her years of services. Then without further ado Mrs. Cuarto herself walked out on stage to huge applause and began to speak:

*cough*Emm...good afternoon children. It makes me sad to be here right now. To say that I'm leaving soon but know that I will miss you all very much. I have seen many writers come

and go. I've seen some raise to fame and others…let it destroy them. I have watched each of you mature in your own unique and special way and I will miss this place so very much and getting to work with each and every one of you.x

While I've seen this company go through heaven and hell, and have stood by its every decision. But I will never condone the creation of THE DEPARTMENTS *loud applause and cheering* *Yes, we have each been forced to conform and mold ourselves to a certain stereotype. It may seem like we are trapped by these stereotypes, like they control our lives in a domineering way. The sad thing is, most people let them. We live our lives in such a way that we are controlled by what other people have thought about our lives.*

*The thing we fail to notice is that these "labels" that control our lives, exist **only in the minds of other people**. Their power exists only if you allow it to. Do not let someone say that you must become a 'normal' type of person; whatever that means. I should think life would be rather dull if we were all 'normal'.*

You must remember, and I will argue this, that beauty is not measured by something we as humans have labeled and mistaken for 'physical attraction'. Beauty is measured by how distinctively unique you are from everyone else. And everyone of us has this beauty deep down inside.

*I know that my salute is short but I know that if I continue any longer*starts to pull out hankie, eyes watered over, voice quivering*I won't be able to go on. I need to get this over with soon. So in conclusion…you can offer your fellow man the best kind of freedom. Do not condemn him with a label but allow him to live freely, just as he was born.*

For we are all born into this world without a label and by God, we better make our way out without any. *Steps back from podium bursting into tears, hugs the editor, people are standing on their feet applauding, and whistling.*

Raquel found that she was tearing up a bit. She loved Ms. Cuarto's speech. The idea that people could escape being a slave to a label, to an idea, to what people thought about you…

She suddenly collided with a young man who was exiting the MA. "Oh my gosh, excuse me..."

The young man only chuckled. "No worries my dear."

It took Raquel a second to know whom she was speaking with. "You're...Christian Martinez..." She was absolutely dumbstruck.

"Oh you appear to be an aficionado. Miss..."

"Oh, yeah, um... Polanski. Raquel Polanski." She found herself to be

"Pleasure to make your acquaintance Miss Polanski." Christian offered a friendly hand. "I take it you're the tenderfoot of the offices?"

"Oh well, I actually just arrived in New York today."

"Beg your pardon, but are you staying with anybody in New York?"

"I'm afraid not Mr. Martinez. I don't really know anybody at all here."

The young author shook his head. "We must adjust that then, musn't we?" He slowly reached into a jacket pocket to retrieve a silver envelope. "I'm throwing a really big New Year's Party and it would be a pleasure, I assure you Miss Polanski, if you graced us with your presence there."

Raquel was delighted, "Oh, it would be my pleasure!"

"Splendid!" The young man cried out among the crowd of moving authors. "I've never thrown a New Year's Party before, but I will make this first time the best. After all," he looked down at Raquel with a slight twinkling in his eye, "The most excitable things happen at New Year's Parties."

*   *   *

"Police reported a shootout last night in the Ironwood Press Headquarters located near the financial district. The unfortunate battle occurred between Ironwood Press CEO Mitchell Schuler, the FBI's most wanted hit-man Samuel Schiano and two FBI agents. Also involved were renowned author Christian Martinez and an aspiring author Raquel Polanski. According to reports, the shootout began when Polanski was reportedly abducted by Schiano and Schuler who planned to murder her. They took Polanski to one of the higher levels of the building and were surprised by an attack by Martinez, who attempted to rescue Polanski on his own. It was at that time, that FBI agents Kyle Williams and James Rivers both stormed the building seeking Schiano. Both had been tracking Schiano for the past months and had just recently discovered his whereabouts in New York City. According to investigators Schiano had recently been contracted by Schuler to locate Polanski, a native of Tucson who had recently come to New York in order to sign a contract with Ironwood Press."

"In the shootout, Schuler shot Schiano who was mortally wounded and Polanski several times. She was airlifted to St. Matthew's Presbyterian Hospital with several abdominal gunshot wounds. Doctors say she is now in steady condition. Meanwhile Ironwood Press offices are declared closed with the ongoing investigations…"

The screen cut to a young FBI Agent with his hair matted by sweat recounted various parts of the story. "We immediately went in suspecting that Schiano was the only one armed…"

It cut again, this time to a young man walking hurriedly along, a million different mics poised in his face and just as many questions being hurled at him.

"Mr. Martinez, what exactly happened up there?"

"Why would Schuler want to kill this girl?"

"What do you suspect the motive was?"

"Why did you try to save the girl?"

"What is your relationship to her?"

But he continued along with an unwavering face and the constant steam of his breath, vanishing in small wisps before him.

He looks really familiar. Who is that? Through the haze of her vision Raquel could just make out the figures that flashed by on the t.v. in her hospital room. Slowly her eyes began to open to allowing the rush of life's colors to return to her eyes.

"Ah, I never thought you would awaken."

Never before in the expanse of so many weeks had she been more glad to hear that voice.

Sitting right beside the hospital bed was Christian Martinez. He's suit was rumpled, his eyes completely bloodshot, and the once neat clump of hair had become a shocking mess. A giant smile found its way across his lips.

"Oh my God, Christian!" Raquel felt herself trying to rise up from the bed but found that the pain rendered her body totally motionless. She let out a soft groan as the pains in her abdomen flared up.

"No, don't try to rise. You'll be fine."

Raquel laid down again, powerless to move. "Christian, I thought I'd never see you again…"

"Nurse, nurse!" Christian was up and shouting.

A lady appeared in the doorway. "Oh thank God, it's Dina the night nurse. Quickly, my friend here needs assistance!"

Those were the last few words Raquel remembered before she sunk beneath consciousness again.

It didn't seem but a few minutes before she awoke again and saw Christian resting in a chair facing the hospital room window. It seemed as though he sat contemplating everything that had occurred beforehand. The city outside was tinged in a deep purple.

"Christian..."

He quickly looked over at her. In a matter of seconds he was beside her. "Raquel, the doctors report that you are progressing just fine..."

She shook her head lightly. "That's not what I was worried about. It was maybe the fact that I wouldn't see you. It was just that in that moment with Schuler I thought that was the end."

"I admit I felt the same way, Miss Polanski, yet I must say that what you said to that old bastard was, astonishing to say the least."

For a moment they were both completely silent. Raquel took a quick look towards the window. The purple hue that blanketed the city slowly gave way to a softer pink.

"Is it morning?"

"I'm afraid it is Raquel, however the doctor has ordered that you get as much rest as possible. I must call Dina in." Christian from his chair to contact a nurse for Raquel when she began to speak again.

"What were you thinking about?"

"What   do   you   mean?"
"You know, just right now when you were looking outside the window."

"I suppose I was contemplating what you and Schuler had said, to each other."

"It was kinda cheesy I know…"

"Raquel, don't say that. I believe what you had said to him was utterly astounding. You see I had been contemplating it all for a very long time."

"For what, a long time?"

"Oh you know, the whole assassin deal, how the company was being worked, and the philosophies of Mr. Schuler. You see, Mr. Schuler only decided to run the company with the same mechanism that makes society tick. Everything and everyone must have a natural place. You see the whole idea was that the society you were born in to would decide what role you got to play. It all started when you were born, oh yes, at the moment you emerged from the safety of your mother's womb and that first cry of life escaped your lips, it was all decided for you. At that moment you were dammed to the part. If you were a boy you'd grow up to become that everlasting cornerstone of a family, the unwavering rock that never wore its emotions out on his sleeves; if you were a girl you would grow up to become the nurturer of the family and the insubordinate of men. But not all of us were born that way, Raquel."

"Maybe not all of us are meant to be that everlasting cornerstone or that nurturer of the family. You see we are all so vastly different it is not very plausible that people and the mold society grants them is one in the same. Because society does care so much for people as it does for a *certain type* of product. But I refuse to allow society to define people by some stereotype granted by long-standing notions. And I hate the word *normal*. What a dangerous word to the world of mankind. And who is it that may decide what *normal* is. I can no longer live with it. I feel as though I must strip the very hinges of it, destroy it, and rid everyone of any idea on what may be *normal*."

"But to tell you the truth Raquel, I am not sure such a thing will ever come to pass in my life time. Like you said we can't really change the whole of society, in fact I have very little control over the circumstances I find myself involved in. But I can change how I react to it."

"I shall be the defender of the misfits and the freaks. Of the sinners and the mystics, and everyone who ever felt as though they did not belong somewhere in their entire lives. We shall be the champions of the broken-hearted and the hated. We will build a refuge for the rebellious and the unloved. I will embrace all the washed-up, left behind pieces of humanity that seem to have been forgotten."

Christian had quickly pushed a button and Dina had appeared in the doorway. She quietly nodded to Christian and said, "I'll get her to sleep."

Raquel hazily tried to focus on the last of Christian's words as the nurse injected something into the IV. From her bed, the last glimpse of morning sunlight crept through and had shown its magnificent brightness. And she fell asleep, finding rest at last in the depths of overwhelming sleep.

THE END
(well, of that story anyways...)

16366717R00141

Made in the USA
San Bernardino, CA
30 October 2014